There was no moon. The shadowed suburban street was quiet. Neat lawns and disciplined flower beds surrounded darkened houses. In the distance a dog barked once, then was silent.

The battered station wagon, lights off, coasted to a stop in front of a house in the middle of the block. Fallen leaves scrunched under its tires. A striped cat, patrolling her territory, darted under a sheltering bush to watch the intruders.

The two men were efficient. They didn't speak, but one grunted with the weight as they unloaded the first of two wrapped objects from the vehicle.

There was a subdued crackle of plastic as they removed the outsize rubbish bags. The taller of the two men fussed over the exact positioning of the bodies on the damp grass.

When he was satisfied, he looked up at the house. "Traitor," he said softly.

As they drove away, the lawn sprinkler system came to life with a sibilant hiss.

INNER CIRCLE

THE 8TH DETECTIVE INSPECTOR CAROL ASHTON MYSTERY

Claire McNab

THE NAIAD PRESS, INC.
1999

Printed in the United States of America on acid-free paper
First Edition
First Printing September, 1996
Second Printing February, 1997
Third Printing April, 1999

Editor: Lisa Epson
Cover designer: Bonnie Liss (Phoenix Graphics)
Typesetter: Sandi Stancil

Library of Congress Cataloging-in-Publication Data

McNab, Claire.
    Inner circle / Claire McNab.
        p.   cm.
    ISBN 1-56280-135-X (pbk.)
    I. Title. II. Series: McNab, Claire. Detective Inspector Carol
Ashton mystery : 8.
PS3563.C3877I56   1996
813'.54—dc20   96-26687
                                                              CIP

For Sheila

ACKNOWLEDGMENTS

Special thanks to Greg Simpson; to my valued friend, Sue Martin; to my excellent editor, Lisa Epson; and finally, to Sandi Stancil, whose skill and patience are monumental.

ABOUT THE AUTHOR

CLAIRE MCNAB is the author of ten Detective Inspector Carol Ashton mysteries: *Lessons in Murder, Fatal Reunion, Death Down Under, Cop Out, Dead Certain, Body Guard, Double Bluff, Inner Circle, Chain Letter* and *Past Due*. She has also written two romances, *Under the Southern Cross* and *Silent Heart*.

While pursuing a career as a high school teacher in Sydney, she began her writing career with comedy plays and textbooks. She left teaching in the mid-eighties to become a full-time writer. In her native Australia she is known for her self-help and children's books.

For reasons of the heart now permanently resident in the United States, Claire teaches fiction writing in the UCLA Extension Writers' Program. She returns to Australia at least once a year to refresh her Aussie accent.

PROLOGUE

There was no moon. The shadowed suburban street was quiet. Neat lawns and disciplined flower beds surrounded darkened houses. In the distance a dog barked once, then was silent.

The battered station wagon, lights off, coasted to a stop in front of a house in the middle of the block. Fallen leaves scrunched under its tires. A striped cat, patrolling her territory, darted under a sheltering bush to watch the intruders.

The two men were efficient. They didn't speak,

but one grunted with the weight as they unloaded the first of two wrapped objects from the vehicle.

There was a subdued crackle of plastic as they removed the outsize rubbish bags. The taller of the two men fussed over the exact positioning of the bodies on the damp grass.

When he was satisfied, he looked up at the house. "Traitor," he said softly.

As they drove away, the lawn sprinkler system came to life with a sibilant hiss.

CHAPTER ONE

Detective Sergeant Mark Bourke squinted as he ducked under the blue-and-white plastic tape that delineated the crime scene. The autumn nights were cool, but the sun still had a bite, even this early in the morning. Although most of tree-lined Burma Drive had been cordoned off, curious onlookers were at all vantage points, some locals equipped with binoculars.

Bourke looked back at the crush of media vehicles. Reporters clustered around the police doctor, who was trying to make his way to his car. Bourke's blunt-featured face, usually pleasant, clenched in a scowl. Gesturing to a uniformed officer, he snapped, "Keep them back. Way back. And don't let any media talk their way into these neighboring houses."

The constable looked doubtfully at the swelling crowd. "We'll try, but —"

"Just do it."

The focus of police activity was at the lower edge of an unfenced gently sloping lawn, freshly cut and still a lush green, even after a long, hot summer. White screens shielded the crime scene from the media's cameras. On the right side of the lawn a short driveway led up to a double garage. Wide sandstone steps continued to the substantial, but undistinguished, house. Its single story of pale brick was capped with a brown tiled roof. Some attempt to mitigate its plainness had been made with a number of sandstone urns spilling bright cascades of flowers. The beige front door was tightly closed, although Bourke was sure the white curtains twitched in the front room.

He glared balefully at a news helicopter chattering overhead, then turned his attention to the crime scene. The photographer was packing up his gear and telling a long involved joke to one of the forensic technicians. They laughed together, ignoring the still faces turned to the sky, the flies that were beginning to buzz around the scent of death.

The bodies were laid out precisely on the grass, their arms folded tight behind them, their feet bound. Each wore jeans and a bloody T-shirt. The younger man, his mouth gaping below the black cloth of his blindfold, lay parallel to the roadway to form the top

4

of the *T* shape; the older, stockier male formed the stem of the letter. His mouth was closed tightly, as though he had met with fortitude the bullets that had shattered his chest. A rolled newspaper rested against his thigh.

"Quite a shock for the guy delivering the paper," said Bourke to Liz Carey, head of the crime scene team. "Don't imagine the rest of the street got their Monday morning news in time for breakfast."

Short and square, with a shock of iron-gray hair, Liz grinned up at Bourke. "Have you seen the headline? Seems appropriate."

He leaned over to inspect the rolled newspaper. The black lettering was clear: DEATH PENALTY DEMAND. Underneath in smaller print it continued: *Agar Blasts Critics. 'Let the People's Will Be Heard'.*

"He's pissing into the wind," said Liz. "They'll never reinstate the death penalty."

"Mr. Agar thinks he can say or do anything," said Bourke, his voice heavy with scorn. He glanced up at the house. "I bet he's waiting for the timing to be just right before he fronts the cameras."

"He's a politician, so he can't help it, but even he would think twice before using this for publicity."

Bourke shoved his hands into his pockets. "You think so? It looks like every media outlet got the word something was happening here."

Liz grinned at his sharp tone. "Inspector Ashton on her way? That'll stir them up even more." She gestured toward the carefully arranged bodies. "And I can only imagine what reporters are going to make of this little layout. Got any ideas?"

Brushing a fly away from his face, Bourke said irritably, "Beats me. Some ritual . . . An initial?"

5

Liz looked at him sideways. "Not your usual sunny self, Mark?"

He grunted. There was a flurry of excitement in the media contingent. The sunlight caught a sweep of smooth blonde hair. Bourke watched Carol Ashton stride gracefully through the crowd, nodding recognition to reporters, but never breaking step. They'd worked together for years and he respected her, both as a friend and as a colleague, but sometimes, seeing her approaching like this, her cool beauty took him by surprise. She looked purposeful, determined, professional — all the things he knew her to be — but he also knew her well enough to see the anger in the tightness of her jaw and the line of her mouth.

Carol made a face as she came up to them. "You could have warned me about the media blitz."

Liz Carey grinned. "Thought you'd be used to it, being as you're so notorious."

Carol's eyes narrowed as she looked up at the house. "Thanks to Agar. Has he made an appearance?"

"Not yet," said Bourke. "Thought I'd leave him to you."

"Thanks a lot." Carol switched her attention to the carefully arranged bodies on the grass.

Liz Carey gestured widely. "Artistic arrangement, eh? I was sure you'd like to see the stiffs before we moved them."

"They were found like this?"

"Absolutely. And no one's moved them, at least since the sprinkler system came on sometime during the night. The grass underneath each body is comparatively dry."

6

"Identification?"

Bourke shook his head. "Not a thing. Someone's cleaned out their pockets."

"Any of the neighbors hear or see anything?"

"I've got a team door-knocking both sides of the street," said Bourke, "but so far nothing. And Anne Newsome's at the local cop shop getting a statement from the guy who discovered the bodies, but I don't think he's going to be much help."

"Liz? What've you got?"

"Pretty well what you see, Carol. Seems they were both tied up, blindfolded, and then shot in the chest. Multiple wounds. Rigor's pretty well established in both bodies, so that makes time of death roughly twelve hours ago." She chuckled. "And I think someone would have noticed if they'd been lying there since yesterday evening, so that means they were brought here sometime after the firing squad."

Carol raised her eyebrows. "Firing squad?"

Liz beckoned Carol to come closer to the younger man's body. Using a ballpoint pen as a pointer, she said, "Look here. You can see the fragments of yellow cloth and a safety pin. Someone pinned cloth targets over their hearts." She indicated a wound in the left shoulder. "Not everyone was a crack shot, however."

"A lot of noise," said Bourke. "Certainly would have woken up the neighborhood if it'd happened locally. I've asked for a check of all the metropolitan stations to see if anyone reported anything that could have been a volley of gunfire."

The three of them stepped aside as two gurneys rumbled along the footpath. "Okay to move them now?" asked Liz.

"Sure." Carol watched as the bodies, grotesquely

7

frozen by rigor mortis, were loaded. She peered at the grass, which still had the imprints of the bodies. "Did you get anything here at the scene?"

"Only this," said Liz, showing Carol a plastic evidence bag. "It's some sort of medallion on a broken chain. Otherwise they were bloody careful. Hope we're luckier with the bodies and the clothing."

There was a stir in the crush of media. Carol looked up. "Surprise," she said. "Kent Agar is making an appearance."

A man had come out of the front door of the house on the rise above them. He was slightly built and wore a well-tailored charcoal double-breasted suit and his signature red bow tie. Agar paused for a long moment — Bourke made a sour observation about grandstanding — then began to walk slowly down the sandstone steps.

Carol met him before he was halfway. "Mr. Agar? I have some questions. Could we go back into the house?"

Agar stopped on the step above her. She was half a head taller, so they were eye to eye. Uncharitably, she decided that he had done this deliberately, knowing the cameras were on them as they spoke. He had a small-featured, sharp fac, and high-arched eyebrows that gave him a habitual expression of supercilious surprise. His thinning auburn hair abruptly reminded Carol of Sybil, and the rich, exuberant red of her hair.

Agar's narrow mouth twisted in a derisive half smile. "Keeping me away from my public, Inspector? Afraid I'll have something disparaging to say about law enforcement . . . or *you*?"

"I would have thought you'd said quite enough

about me... All under parliamentary privilege, I note."

He gave a short laugh at her caustic tone. "You'd sue me if I spoke outside parliament, would you, Inspector? But I only spoke the truth — you *are* a sexual deviate, aren't you? And in my opinion that makes you unfit to take any position of authority." He cocked his head, apparently expecting some reaction.

Carol kept her face blank. "Do you know what time the garden sprinkler system comes on during the night?"

"Changing the subject, Inspector?"

Carol waited. Agar gestured impatiently. "I've no idea. I've just bought this place. I imagine there's a timer somewhere."

"Have you looked at the bodies closely?"

"Of course not." He was clearly affronted. "The first I knew that anything was wrong was when I heard the sirens. I had no intention of joining the ghouls who turned up like flies at a picnic." He gave Carol a small, smug smile. "However, I did call the Commissioner and the Minister for Police... But I suppose you know that already."

Professional distancing always controlled her anger. She said neutrally, "Would you be willing to see if you can identify either of the men?"

"Identify them?" His voice was stiff with indignation. "I imagine the bodies could have been dumped on anyone's property. It's just my bad luck that it happens to be mine."

Carol looked at him steadily. "There is a possibility, however remote, that there is some link to you because of your role as a member of parliament."

"That's highly unlikely." His tone was contemptuous. "You're just trying to involve me in some grubby little drug deal gone wrong."

"It seems odd that two bodies should be arranged so carefully on your particular lawn, Mr. Agar."

He glanced down at the activity below, then back to Carol. "It's hardly common knowledge that I live here, since I only moved in last week. That means this has got nothing to do with me." Bellicose, he shoved his face close to hers. "So, I suggest, Inspector Ashton, that you stop harassing me and get on with your job."

Unmoved, Carol said crisply, "It will only take a moment."

His mouth tightened. "Oh, very well!" He pushed past her and strode down the remaining steps. Halting beside Bourke and Liz Carey, he gave a cursory look at the bodies. Then he jerked his head back. Carol, following, heard him exclaim, "Christ!"

Bourke put a hand under Agar's elbow. "You okay?"

Agar was gray faced. He swayed and bent double. It seemed he would fall without Bourke's support. "Can you take the blindfold off?" His voice was hoarse. "The boy . . ."

Carol took Agar's other arm. "No, that's not possible. It has to be removed later, when the bodies go to the morgue. Do you want to sit down?"

With an obvious effort, Agar straightened. "I'd like to go inside."

Carol said, "You recognize the younger man." It wasn't a question.

Agar nodded slowly. "I'm not sure, but it could be . . ."

"Who?" Bourke was abrupt.

"A friend of my son's. Bayliss. Dean Bayliss. But it can't be . . ."

CHAPTER TWO

Half an hour later, Carol and Bourke walked down the sandstone steps leading from Kent Agar's house. They hadn't been able to interview the politician. Once inside, he'd rushed to the bathroom and they had heard him vomiting. When he returned, pale and shaking, he'd refused to answer any questions and had reacted with spluttering fury when Carol had asked solicitously if there was any reason that he might need personal protection. Agar had announced he was calling his doctor and asked them to leave.

Outside the sun was higher, the day was warmer and, with the removal of the two corpses, the sightseers had dwindled to a tenacious few. The media contingent, however, still lingered.

A flurry of activity greeted their appearance: Cameras were hoisted to shoulders; reporters hastily checked their grooming; microphones were readied.

"They scent blood," said Bourke. "There's no way they didn't see Agar's reaction."

As Carol and Bourke reached the bottom of the drive, several reporters shouted questions. Carol shook her head slightly, indicating that she wouldn't give a sound bite. In the front of the pack, one brashly determined woman seemed energized by this refusal. Brandishing her microphone like a sword, she ducked under the crime-scene tape, evaded a uniformed constable, and rushed at Carol. "Inspector Ashton! How's Kent Agar involved? Did he identify the bodies?"

Carol said smoothly, "I can't comment at the moment. This is obviously very early in the investigation."

The outflanked constable finally managed to grab the reporter's arm. As she was escorted away, she called back over her shoulder, "Inspector, how do you feel about Agar's personal attack on you last week . . . ?"

Carol made no sign she had heard the question. Turning her back on the media, she said to Bourke, "Mark, I'll be taken off the case if Agar's involved in anything but a peripheral way."

"There isn't a cop that doesn't hate his guts after the attacks he's made on the Police Service."

"True, but they were general — the one on me

was personal. It could be hard to believe I wasn't biased after that."

Bourke's mouth curved in a cynical smile. "And you aren't?"

Carol glanced up at Agar's mundane house. "If you mean would I be upset if something unfortunate were to happen to the little bastard, the answer's obviously no. That doesn't mean I can't run an investigation fairly."

"I'd love to nail Agar for something."

There was so much venom in Bourke's voice that Carol was startled. He was easygoing and objective, and rarely let even the most sordid crimes or loathsome suspects disturb his equanimity. "Agar's really got under your skin, hasn't he?"

"I can't imagine why," said Bourke with heavy irony. "I mean, Agar's only a narrow-minded, self-righteous, grade A hypocrite who's an apologist for White Australia, the gun lobby, and any other loony right-wing group who needs someone to make wild accusations under parliamentary privilege."

"Well, you've convinced me!"

He grinned at her dry tone. "Sorry, but I really can't stand the guy."

Carol frowned at the grass where the indentations were still plain. "Any ideas on the *T* formation? I think we can take it that the arrangement was intentional. Can you think of any significance as far as Agar's concerned?"

"Not a thing. As I told Liz, my guess is that it's an initial or a symbol of something. It doesn't have to be a letter of the alphabet — upside down it's just two lines at right angles."

"Inspector?" A young constable, face flushed, hurried up. "I've found out the lawn sprinklers were timed to go on at three-thirty for half an hour... And..." He paused in obvious triumph. "I've found someone who saw the bodies dumped!"

Buoyant with his achievements, he led Bourke and Carol to the house opposite Agar's. It was a pleasantly sprawling building with large picture windows and a faintly neglected air. The rumpled middle-aged man waiting at the top of the short flight of steps hadn't shaved. He introduced himself as he shook hands with Carol. "Hal Brackett, Inspector. As I told the officer, I may have seen something..."

He ushered them inside. The living room was untidy, with newspapers piled beside an easy chair. The coffee table held dirty glasses, a nearly empty bottle of whiskey, and an overflowing ashtray. Brackett looked around. "Sorry about this."

A polite prompt from Bourke, "You may be able to help our investigation?" elicited a weary smile from Brackett.

"It may be nothing..." His voice trailed off. He made an ineffectual gesture at the room. "I never was much good at housekeeping."

After a moment's silence, Carol said, "Mr. Brackett, you saw, or heard, something during the night?"

Brackett sighed. "I told the officer, I haven't been sleeping well... that's why I didn't answer when your people knocked earlier... I'd finally dozed off." He fell silent.

"Mr. Brackett?"

He responded to Carol's cue with another sigh. "This morning, about three-thirty, I got up because I couldn't get to sleep. I came out here in the dark and . . ." He looked at the whiskey bottle. ". . . I had a drink." He added defensively, "Just something to relax me."

"And?"

"I went over to the window and looked out. Not for any particular reason — just for something to do. There was a station wagon, Volvo, dark colored, on the other side of the street. I noticed it because it started to move off without lights, and it stayed that way until it turned the corner at the end of the street."

Carol said, "Can you be sure it was a Volvo wagon? It was dark last night, Mr. Brackett. There was no moon, and there are a lot of trees in this street."

His mouth turned down at the corners. "It was a Volvo," he said bluntly. "My wife . . . my ex-wife drives one. Dirty brown color." A pause, then he added, "I hated that car."

Outside, Bourke made a face at Carol. "I'll check the description of the station wagon against the stolen vehicle listings, but Brackett's been hitting the sauce, so how reliable is he?"

"The time he gives might be elastic, although it would fit in with the lawn sprinklers, since the bodies had to be in place by three-thirty. Regarding the station wagon, I think he disliked that particular model enough to recognize it."

Bourke grinned. "At least he's not suggesting it's his ex-wife driving the getaway car, is he?"

16

"No," said Carol. "Let's hope the thought doesn't occur to him."

Carol's office was standard-issue police utilitarian, with impersonal furniture, neutral walls, and a window providing a view of yet another generic city building. As she entered, the phone rang. On top of the papers on her desk was a message from Superintendent Edgar with an imperious *Urgent* scrawled across the top. She picked up the receiver, expecting the Super's self-important bass.

"Carol?" Madeline's husky voice had a provocative lilt. "Where were you last night? I called, but you weren't home."

"I was working late."

This wasn't strictly true. Carol had found herself uncharacteristically reluctant to go home to an empty house and had spent two hours in a gym working out until she was exhausted.

"I haven't seen you for days." Rather than resentment, Madeline's tone was one of mild astonishment.

"I'll get back to you when I can. Right now I've got an appointment..."

"So you don't have time to hear that the media were tipped off about the bodies on Agar's lawn, *before* the cops were called?"

Carol straightened in her chair. "Are you sure?"

"I've been talking to the news director here at the station." Madeline sounded pleased with herself. "Bill says Channel Thirteen's overnight standby crew arrived at Agar's house about the same time as the first patrol car. That was about six-fifteen. And we weren't the only ones — apart from other networks, key radio stations had been notified too."

"How notified? And when? Was it logged in?"

Madeline gave a low laugh at Carol's crisp questions. "You could see me tonight and learn every detail."

"I need to know now. What's the news director's name?"

Madeline sighed. "Bill Keith, but I can tell you myself . . . It was an anonymous tip-off by phone at five-forty this morning. Whoever it was said that there had been a double murder at Kent Agar's new home on Burma Drive, gave the exact address, and even helpfully supplied the nearest cross street."

"Madeline, I'd appreciate it if you kept this quiet until we check it out. It might just have been a neighbor who didn't want to get involved."

"You mean I can't feature this as a breaking story on my show tonight?" said Madeline in mock outrage. "As it is, we're trying to get Agar on in person, though his PR woman won't give a definite answer yet."

"The Shipley Report" was stripped at seven o'clock, Monday to Friday, and Madeline Shipley was a potent force in television. Her image — copper hair, wide gray eyes, and confident smile — rode on the sides of buses, beamed down from billboards, stared out from the pages of magazines. Her interviewing skills, polished on many high-profile egos, ensured high ratings, and this in turn encouraged public figures to queue to be on her show.

Thinking of how shaken Agar had been when she

and Bourke had left him, Carol said, "Do you really think he'll go on television tonight? A double murder can't be good publicity."

"Darling," said Madeline, "*any* publicity is good publicity to someone like him." Her tone became warmly intimate as she purred, "Am I going to see you after the show? Please don't disappoint me."

Carol was irritated to feel a thrill of desire, and surprised to feel irritation. "I'll get back to you, but it's likely I'll be tied up on this case."

As she put down the receiver Carol reflected that when she was removed from Madeline she felt strong and complete, but in person Madeline had the disquieting ability to put Carol off balance, to jangle and disturb her. It certainly wasn't Madeline's obsessive paranoia about secrecy — that was only an aggravation. And it wasn't just the undoubted potency of Madeline's physical attractiveness. Somehow it was to do with the stainless-steel quality of Madeline's will, her total self-confidence in the efficacy of her palpable charm, and the seductive suggestion that her feelings for Carol provided the only weakness in Madeline's armor against the world.

Putting his head through the door, Bourke said, "No doubt you've got the same royal command from the Super that I found on my desk. It hasn't taken long for Agar's calls to the Minister and the Commissioner to filter down the ranks."

Carol stood up. "Let's get it over with."

"What's the hurry? We know what he's going to say." Bourke beckoned to the young woman standing behind him. "Anne's here to give you a rundown of the statement she got from the guy who found the bodies."

Anne Newsome crackled with energy. Her stocky body was ramrod straight, her short chestnut hair seemed to spring from her head, and her smooth olive skin glowed with health and enthusiasm. Carol felt an affection for the young constable, remembering herself as a green detective, and how anxious she had been to do well.

Carol subsided into her chair. "Okay, Anne, what've you got?"

"The guy from the newsagent — Dave Flint's his name — drives down each street throwing rolled papers onto the appropriate lawns. He hit Burma Drive at a quarter to six and, because Agar's new in the neighborhood, he slowed down and double-checked his list before he lobbed the newspaper. He says he saw the bodies in mid-throw, and almost sideswiped the curb. Got out, took a good look, then grabbed his mobile phone and called the cops."

Carol broke in. "Did he call anyone else?"

"Just the news agency to say he had to stop delivering papers and wait for the cops."

"And he's positive it was six forty-five?"

Anne nodded. "On the dot. Says people turn feral and start calling if their morning paper doesn't arrive in time for breakfast, so he starts his run at five-thirty in order to cover his whole area on schedule. If he doesn't hit Burma Drive by quarter to six, he knows he's in trouble and —"

The phone interrupted the rush of her words. Carol's end of the conversation was brief. "Yes, Mark's with me ... We're on our way."

She slapped down the receiver. "Anne, while we're with the Super, I want you to double-check the time Flint called in. Then start checking all the major

20

newsrooms for press, radio, and TV. I want to know if they got an early tip-off about the bodies on Agar's lawn and, more importantly, exactly *when*."

"What was that about?" Bourke asked as they walked down the corridor to Superintendent Edgar's office.

"Madeline called to say Channel Thirteen got an anonymous call about the bodies at five-forty this morning. That's five minutes before Flint discovered them."

"Madeline Shipley," said Bourke with an admiring grin. "She's got the story by the throat, as usual." He looked sideways at Carol. "I wouldn't like her after *me* — she never gives up."

"Too true." Carol thought wryly how Madeline would use almost any means to get a jump on her opposition. If guile, charm, or subtle intimidation didn't work, she'd call in a favor — there was always someone influential who owed Madeline something.

Bourke, hands in pockets, was whistling thoughtfully to himself. "The call's interesting, but it could just be someone out jogging who saw the bodies and didn't want to get involved."

"If more than Madeline's station got an early warning, then somebody wants fast, intense publicity."

She broke off as they reached Superintendent Edgar's closed door. She knocked sharply and opened it. His office was a step up from Carol's, but still austere. Edgar was seated behind his slightly larger desk. He swiveled in his regulation chair, gestured for them to sit, then regarded them pensively for a long moment.

Carol gazed back impassively. Superintendent

Edgar had never shown brilliance as a detective, but he had worked his way up the ladder by being a consummate player of office politics. Carol knew that she would have his total support just for as long as he thought it prudent. If Edgar decided that being on Carol's side would damage his career in any way he'd distance himself immediately... unless someone superior to him was willing to take the heat.

Carol was keenly aware of the advantage she had in that her mentor throughout her career was now the Commissioner for Police. It had cut both ways. The Commissioner had certainly advised her, guided her — but in return Carol had been given the hot potatoes, the challenging cases that had the potential to short-circuit her career.

"Well, Carol..." Superintendent Edgar had an avuncular smile she didn't trust. "... This is another fine mess you've got yourself into." He put his elbows on his desk and gave Bourke a man-to-man look. "Eh, Mark? What do you think?"

Bourke scowled. "Anything Agar's involved in has got to be trouble."

Edgar smoothed back his silver hair with a thick hand. "The Commissioner's just spoken with me," he said with satisfaction. "We had a long talk about the situation." He paused to let his audience appreciate his favored status. "I don't have to tell you this one has to be handled with kid gloves. As you say, Mark, Agar is trouble, and he'll be just waiting for us to put a foot wrong. Even so, I'm sure his involvement is only incidental."

He waited, silver eyebrows raised, for acceptance of this view.

Carol said, "There may be evidence that the media were informed before we were, to ensure maximum publicity."

This clearly displeased Edgar. "You're not suggesting Agar is responsible, are you?"

"The whole thing was premeditated. The bodies were brought to the house and deliberately arranged in a pattern on the grass. It seems unlikely it was an accident it was Agar's place."

Frowning, Edgar settled back in his chair. "I want to be kept informed, down to the smallest detail. And I want a clamp on this — no cozy off-the-record chats to reporters, understand?" He tapped his stubby fingers on the arm of his chair. "When are the post-mortems scheduled?"

"Tomorrow morning," said Carol.

"I don't want any leaks there, either. Sometimes the bloody reporters seem to have the autopsy findings before we do."

"We may have a tentative identification of one body," Carol said. "Kent Agar thought he recognized the younger man as a friend of his son's."

The Superintendent's frown deepened at this further unwelcome news. "I don't need to tell you that this investigation could be a minefield. But of course I have every confidence in you both." He sucked in his lips. "I'm hoping you'll find that Agar has no involvement, other than that someone randomly dumped the bodies on his property."

To Carol the subtext was plain: Close the case as quickly and neatly as possible with the least political fallout.

"If Agar's spot-on with his identification," said

Bourke, "there's got to be some tie-in. It's too much to believe that a friend of Agar's son turns up dead at Agar's Sydney house."

"In the eventuality that Agar's heavily involved," said Edgar tartly, "Carol's off the case. After the press we've had lately, we can't afford any suggestion of prejudice on the investigating officer's part."

Carol didn't argue. On one level the possibility of being replaced infuriated her: She wanted to be the nemesis of whoever had coldbloodedly ordered the executions. However, as far as her personal life was concerned, freedom from the pressures of this investigation would be an advantage. Sybil was arriving from overseas in a little over a week's time, and Carol didn't want to be consumed by a high-profile case.

It was as if Bourke had read her thoughts. As he closed the door to Edgar's office, he said, "Sybil's been in London for well over a year, hasn't she? Pat was asking the other night when she's coming home."

"Sometime next week. Why?"

Her hard tone made him put up his hands in mock defense. "Hey, Carol, just an innocent question. No hidden agenda, honest!"

She gave him a apologetic smile. Bourke and his wife, Pat, were good friends. "Sorry, Mark. I've no idea why I'm so touchy."

Of course she knew. Her life was changing — *she* was changing. Her work had once satisfied her fully. Relationships had been pushed to the side ... important, but not central to her happiness. Now she felt impelled to find a balance, to make decisions that she would have avoided in the past.

Sometimes it seemed to her that only when she

was running early in the morning did she achieve harmony between her mind and body. Then she occasionally felt a flash of joy — a conviction that the future was full of opportunity and achievement. The quick thud of her feet on the dirt track, the beauty of the wild bushland, the amiable company of her neighbor's German shepherd — all these could combine to calm her roiling thoughts and ease the tension that tightened her shoulders during her working day.

Sybil's return to Australia was the issue that was forcing this reevaluation. Although they had both acknowledged that there were no strings, that each was free to do whatever she wished, Carol knew that until she saw Sybil, she couldn't make any hard decisions about the future.

CHAPTER THREE

When Bourke and Carol met at the city morgue the next morning, both victims had names. Agar's hesitant identification had been confirmed by Dean Bayliss's father, who had been flown to Sydney by police helicopter in the late afternoon. At first he had insisted it wasn't his son, repeating this over and over while tears streamed down his cheeks. At last, shoulders slumped, he nodded acquiescence. "It's Dean."

He'd looked at Carol, his lips trembling. "I

haven't seen much of him lately. I mean, he's moved out and what with one thing and another..." His voice trailed away.

Carol had said the soothing, meaningless words expected at moments like this, masking the real gut-wrenching sympathy she felt for the man. With a stab of guilt she thought of her own son, David. Her ex-husband had never made any difficulty about visitation rights, but recently there'd been occasions when Carol had limited the time she'd spent with David because of pressures from her work.

She loved David so much and treasured his company, yet somehow she could always find excuses to let her job come first. As soon as she had arranged for Mr. Bayliss's return to Katamulla, she had called her ex-husband's home. "Eleanor, I know it's short notice, but I wonder if I could see David sometime this coming weekend..." She genuinely liked Justin's second wife, so felt quite free to express her laughing embarrassment when Eleanor reminded her that David had a long-anticipated soccer camp both Saturday and Sunday. "Of course, I'd forgotten. He did tell me all about it... in exhaustive detail."

As she put down the receiver Carol thought ruefully that she had only half-listened when David had enthused about the soccer camp. She pictured his animated face, his green eyes so like hers, his straight fair hair falling across his forehead. When she and Justin had divorced he had been a little boy. It seemed to her that she had hardly noticed him growing older, taller. Now he was twelve. In a few short years he would be Dean Bayliss's age, launching himself into adult life. What influence had she had on her son? She knew he loved her, but what did he really think of her?

Her thoughts had been interrupted by Bourke, who had a name to attach to the second body. The older victim had been identified by his fingerprints. Wayne Bucci had had two convictions, each involving the possession of explosives suspected of being stolen. In the first case he'd received a suspended sentence, but the second offense put him behind bars for several months in a country jail.

Further information had been faxed from Bathurst early that morning, and Carol studied the pages while she and Bourke waited for the pathologist. The arrest photographs showed a powerfully built, balding man with a hard expression. His mouth compressed, he stared a challenge at the camera. Carol wondered if he'd met his death with the same resolve.

Bourke had brought a morning newspaper to the morgue. He thrust it at Carol. "See the front page?"

"I read it over breakfast."

"Every news outlet Anne checked yesterday had been tipped off about the bodies," said Bourke. "All the calls were anonymous, but made by at least two different people — a man and a woman. I'd love to think Agar was involved in getting the media stirred up, but I can't see why he'd do it, since it's hardly positive publicity."

Black banner headlines declared: M.P. IN DOUBLE DEATH PUZZLE. The following story was light on facts but heavy on speculation about the killings, which were variously attributed to gang warfare, a drug deal gone wrong and, in the most sensational hypothesis, that these were the first victims of a neophyte serial killer who had arranged the bodies in a *T* formation to give the initial letter of a word that later victims would spell out in its entirety.

Dean Bayliss was named and a photograph of him and his parents included. Much had been made of the fact that he came from Kent Agar's hometown but, as Agar had been uncharacteristically unavailable for comment, there were only vague conjectures as to what significance this might have.

Wayne Bucci was referred to as a mystery victim, for whom no next of kin had yet been located.

The article encapsulated Agar's career... *to some a crusader for traditional values, to others a dangerous right-wing extremist*... with a posed photograph taken at a flattering angle. There was also a photo of Carol and Agar meeting on the steps of his house. Near the end of the article, the journalist declared, *A reliable source advises that Detective Inspector Carol Ashton has asked to be removed from the case because of a perceived conflict of interest.*

Bourke tapped this section of the article with a forefinger. "Wasn't me, ma'am," he said with exaggerated humility. "Besides, I'm not a bit reliable."

"The good old anonymous source," said Carol with a dry smile. "What would any self-respecting journalist do without such a device when making up a quote?"

"I didn't see Agar on 'The Shipley Report' last night," said Bourke. "Unusual for him to pass up an opportunity to dazzle."

"He's on tonight," said Carol. Madeline had left a message on Carol's machine at home with this information, plus an acid comment on Carol's unavailability. It had been very late, and Carol hadn't called back.

"Carol! Mark!" boomed a hearty voice. "So sorry to keep you waiting. Had the usual family crisis at breakfast." The pathologist, Jeff Duke, was a cheerfully bombastic family man. He had six children — and a growing brood of grandchildren — an expanding waistline, and a gratifyingly meticulous approach to his job.

Dressed in faded green scrubs, he led the way down the stark corridor, all the while talking over his shoulder. "My youngest son, Brad, has just announced he wants to be a cop. His mother's totally flipped. Since the last Royal Commission she thinks law enforcement's the slippery path to graft and corruption." He guffawed. " 'Thelma,' I said, 'that's the way of the world — everyone's out for number one, and at least he'll make a good living.' It didn't go down well."

While Mark made an appropriate response, Carol tried not to breathe deeply. However often her duty brought her to the morgue, she could never get used to the pervasive, ever-present odors of bodily fluids combined with the pungent smells of disinfectants and preservatives.

Dr. Duke opened a door and ushered them into a coldly functional room. His assistant, a prematurely balding man with bulging eyes, nodded a greeting. One wall was taken up by banks of stainless-steel refrigerator doors, each large enough to accommodate a cadaver on a tray.

Two corpses lay ready for the pathologist, each face up on a plastic body tray. Yesterday both had taken a journey on a jolting gurney to be labeled, photographed, fingerprinted, undressed, weighed, and X-rayed. Now they awaited the final bodily indignities the medical profession could provide.

Side by side, naked, Dean Bayliss and Wayne Bucci waited indifferently. The husky physique and heavy body hair of the older man contrasted with the trim, athletic physique of the nineteen-year-old. The stiffness of rigor mortis had ebbed as the inevitable processes of degeneration continued, so the arms that had previously been frozen behind each man now lay slackly beside them.

Before approaching the bodies, Carol and Bourke put on paper gowns, paper masks, and paper overshoes. Duke strapped on a full-length rubber apron. Snapping on latex gloves, he said, "I had a preliminary look at both of them last night when I took blood samples. I don't think there's any doubt about the cause of death, and lividity indicates that after death they were laid on their backs and left there for transport." He nodded to his assistant. "We'll do the boy first."

With one easy movement they swung Dean Bayliss to the hollowed surface of a stainless-steel table that had gutters to carry fluids away to drainage holes. "Theatrical murder," Duke said, "but not all of them were good shots." He indicated dried blood at the left shoulder and arm. "Some missed the heart completely." Flicking a gloved finger at the corpse's tanned chest, he added, "I've no doubt I'll find fragments of yellow cloth deep in the tissues."

Bourke grimaced. "Trussed up like a chicken, targeted, and then shot."

Both victims had had bright yellow cotton circles pinned over their hearts before they had been killed.

31

Carol looked at the young man's face. Only nineteen. Perhaps in those last moments he'd thought it was a game meant to frighten him. Or had he known that he was about to die, that his heart was pulsing its last beats? She imagined if it had been her: Would she have called out, argued, begged for mercy?

In life Dean Bayliss would have been handsome, with regular features and thick brown hair. Carol could imagine him laughing, moving with the grace of youth. Now he was a corpse with no pride left, about to be expertly butchered, his organs examined, weighed, sampled, and his shattered chest probed for evidence. His face was ashen, and now that the blindfold had been removed his dull eyes stared at the fluorescent lights on the stained ceiling.

The pathologist switched on the voice-activated recorder and came around the table to stand beside Carol. "See the marks here on his wrist? It's mirrored on his other arm. He struggled hard, but was securely tied. Same with the other guy." He indicated the corpse's neck. "And those abrasions there on his throat . . . seem to indicate that he was secured so he couldn't slump forward."

Bourke took out his notebook. "We don't want the prisoner botching his execution," he said dryly. "He's a much cleaner target if he stands straight."

"I imagine he was sitting," said Duke. "Your legs tend to give out when you're helpless and you know you're about to be killed."

A round-faced young woman in green scrubs put her head around the door of the examining room. "Inspector Ashton? There's an urgent call for you."

Carol gestured at the wall phone. "I'll take it here."

"You can't." She seemed delighted to add, "They told me to say you had to take it privately."

"Use my room," said Duke.

Carol stripped off her mask, gown, and overshoes and left them on a bench by the door.

"This way," said the young woman. From the way she looked at Carol it was obvious that the call had piqued avid curiosity. "I suppose it's because a member of parliament's involved . . ." she said, letting her voice trail off expectantly.

Carol smiled pleasantly. "What's your name?"

She looked momentarily confused. "My name?"

"We haven't met before, have we?"

"No, I don't think so. I'm Dr. Price. Jeanine Price."

They reached the chief pathologist's untidy office. "Thank you," said Carol. She waited. The young doctor hesitated, then smiled quickly and hurried off. Carol watched her until she was well down the bare corridor before opening the door.

Dr. Duke's room was closer to a large cubicle than an office. Three of the walls were half-glass partitioning and almost all the threadbare brown carpet was covered by furniture: a scarred wooden desk where family photographs jostled with piles of papers; a worn leather chair with a sagging seat; two gray metal bookcases bulging with files and reference books.

Positioning herself in the chair to avoid a broken spring, Carol located the phone under a collapsing heap of folders. "This is Carol Ashton. You have a call for me."

After a moment a neutral male voice said, "Is that Inspector Ashton?"

33

"It is."

"As a security check, please give your mother's family name."

Raising her eyebrows, Carol complied.

"Thank you. Hold, please."

There was a click, and then a new voice. "It's Denise, Carol. Do I have to say more, or is that enough for you to identify me?"

Carol smiled. "You'd be difficult to forget."

Denise Cleever chuckled. "So reassuring. I was afraid you'd say, Who?"

Intrigued that ASIO — Australian Security Intelligence Organization — had contacted her, Carol said, "I presume you want me to call you back on a secure phone?"

"On the ball, as always. Use a pay phone. Here's the number . . ."

Conversations on the public phones in the morgue lobby could be easily overheard, so Carol retrieved her handbag and went out into the mean inner-city streets, walking half a block before she found a phone box. There was rubbish on the floor, graffiti scrawled on the walls, and a smell that seemed a blend of sweat and urine. The phone itself was in working order, although the handset was sticky with some unidentifiable substance. She dialed the number she had been given and in a few moments she had the ASIO agent on the line.

Raising her voice above the sustained roar of the traffic rumbling past, Carol said, "Okay, why are we playing spies?"

Denise Cleever was all business. "You've identified

both the victims in the double murder case you're investigating."

"Yes. Dean Bayliss and Wayne Bucci. One's a teenager from the country and the other's a petty criminal." Carol frowned. "There's a national-security angle?"

"You might say that. Bucci was one of ours."

"Undercover?"

"Very. One of our very best. We need to meet urgently. There's a lot you should know before you get any deeper into your investigation. I'm flying up from Canberra and I'll contact you as soon as I arrive." She gave a short laugh. "And it may sound melodramatic, but we haven't had this conversation. Okay?"

Carol replaced the grubby handset and rubbed her hands on a handkerchief. ASIO's involvement could be a very unwelcome complication, but she was pleased to be seeing Denise Cleever again. A consummate professional, Denise had been involved with Carol on a previous case, and Carol knew she could depend on her to be straightforward and supportive. In a way, each of them shared the same career situation: Working in what was still in many ways a boys' club, it was necessary to be smarter, tougher, and more wary than male colleagues.

As she walked back to the anonymous building that housed the morgue, Carol considered Wayne Bucci in a new light. In the space of a short telephone conversation he had gone from an insignificant receiver of stolen property to an elite undercover ASIO agent. The sketchy details she had about him were almost certainly false, as was his name — they would have been part of his cover. She thought with a pang that his close relatives must now know from ASIO that he was dead, but be unable to do anything to claim his body.

Why would Bucci be murdered in the company of a country teenager who on first reports seemed to have an ordinary, unremarkable life? As soon as Agar had made his tentative identification, Carol had spoken to Sergeant Griffin, the highest ranking officer in the small town of Katamulla. The sergeant seemed unimpressed to have an inspector from the big city calling. "Dean Bayliss?" he'd said dubiously. "Went to school with my son. I reckon you'd be barking up the wrong tree. I'd say, for sure, Dean would be at the bakery right now."

Within ten minutes Sergeant Griffin had called back. His voice held none of his former skepticism. "Inspector Ashton? I hate to say it, but you could be onto something. Dean's not at work, and no one knows where he is. It isn't like him. Not like him at all."

"What is Dean like?"

The sergeant had been emphatic. "A decent young bloke, not like some of them. Left school, got a job, and kept it." He'd become brusque when Carol asked about possible involvement with drugs. "None of that stuff in *my* town. I run a tight ship, know what I mean? Sometimes there's a bit of marijuana, but you can't stop that. Nothing hard — I'd know."

After Bayliss Senior had made the positive identification of his son, Carol had asked Bourke to call Griffin again, saying sardonically that the sergeant might respond to a man-to-man approach;

however, even Bourke's pleasantly persistent questioning had elicited few further details. Bourke had arranged for a photograph of the other victim to be faxed to the sergeant and had asked him to find out when Dean Bayliss — and Bucci, if he had been in Katamulla — had last been seen.

Carol puzzled over what possible link there could be between Kent Agar and the murders. There had to be something — it was hardly blind chance that the bodies of a friend of his son's and an undercover agent had been dumped at the politician's house.

Agar was rabidly right-wing and vehemently supported what he trumpeted as *a return to true family values.* He seemed to believe that this goal would be achieved by attacking minorities — especially gays — limiting social services, severely restricting immigration, banning abortion, liberalizing gun ownership laws, and removing environmental safeguards. His tirades against soft criminal sentencing and what he declared was widespread corruption in law enforcement might conceivably be related to the bodies on his lawn, but as Agar operated in the arena of New South Wales state government, Carol wondered what connection there might be between his preoccupations and Australia's national security.

At the morgue's entrance Carol hesitated. A thin wind blew gritty dust against her face, but she was still reluctant to go inside. From experience she knew the steps the pathologist had taken in her absence. He had made a careful exterior examination of the body, recording his findings as he went. He and his assistant had photographed, measured, and described any injuries, which had then been noted on a body-outline diagram. All orifices had been probed and swabbed. Fingernail scrapings and samples of bodily hair had been sealed in labeled containers.

Next was the internal examination of the body. Even after attending so many post-mortems, Carol could not entirely distance herself from the final violation of what had been a person. She was always careful to appear professionally indifferent, but sometimes she wondered if others, however dispassionate — even callous — they seemed, were feeling the same disturbing emotions.

Back in the examining room, she picked up her discarded paper gown and mask. Bourke gave her an interrogative look. "Nothing important, Mark."

She glanced over at Bucci's body. ASIO would respond to the death of an agent in the field the way the Police Service did when one of their own was taken out — with a concentrated effort that would utilize whatever staff, time, and facilities were necessary for as long as it took.

The pathologist was putting on goggles and a double mask in preparation for accomplished butchery. "Well, Carol, you're back just in time for the best part," he said jovially.

Taking a scalpel, he made a huge Y-shaped incision from throat to crotch. He swiftly cut through the rib cage, the shears making a series of crisp crunching sounds, until he had exposed the contents of the chest.

"Look at this — massive damage. Death would have been instantaneous." Checking X rays displayed on an illuminated panel, he probed the cavity. The bullet made a metallic click as he deposited it in a bowl. "There's one." He gave details to the voice-activated recorder. Probing again, he said, "And another one." He turned it in the forceps. "I'm no expert, but this looks like a different caliber." He went back to the open chest. "Some went right through him, but there's one lodged under the skin of his back and there are fragments where others have shattered."

With neat, economical movements he divided tissue until he could lift out the entire throat and chest contents as a unit. He placed them on an adjoining metal table for later detailed dissection. In the same way the abdominal contents were examined and removed. Gutted, Bayliss stared up at the lights above him.

Then the body was neatly scalped, the hair and skin peeled away from the bone of his skull and pushed down in a grotesque fringe over his face. Carol listened to the buzz of the electric saw, smelt the acrid scent of burning bone dust, thought of Bayliss's weeping father.

Dr. Duke lifted off the top of the skull and peered in at the brain. She hoped that Dean's father had no concept of what a post-mortem involved. When it was completed his son's body would be restored to apparent normality, the top of his skull replaced, the scalp pulled back, the gashed trunk sewn up.

Carol looked at the pathologist bending over the body. Dean Bayliss would be released to his family for the formality of funeral services, the solace of ritual. A post-mortem was a ritual too, but comfort wasn't the objective.

Carol felt a sudden burning anger. What if it had been her son, her David, lying there hollowed, his organs spread out on a table beside him?

Only if she did her job well did this grotesque ritual have a purpose. Justice. Justice for the dead.

CHAPTER FOUR

Denise Cleever, newly arrived from Canberra, called to give Carol details of their meeting later that afternoon, a meeting she was to mention to no one. "Gosh," said Carol, grinning, "do I bring my false mustache and trench coat too?"

"Just yourself, Carol, but follow instructions. You *can* call yourself Agent 99 if you like."

Carol's smile faded as she hung up. The impact the murder of Bucci would have on the investigation would be apparent once she'd discussed the situation with Denise, and the extent of ASIO's participation would determine if Carol would be replaced by someone of higher rank.

Perversely, even after convincing herself earlier that morning that freedom from this particular case would be an advantage, she realized that she now actively wanted to stay in charge.

She turned back to the preliminary forensic report Liz Carey had just had delivered to Carol's desk. The fibers and dust on both sets of clothes contained vegetable matter, possibly from stored hay and rodent droppings. The bright yellow targets had been cut by hand from a piece of cheap cotton material. The blindfolds were a cotton/polyester blend, also roughly cut from a larger section of cloth. The thin nylon rope that bound the ankles and wrists of each victim was widely available throughout the country, generally marketed as a lightweight tow rope for motorists. The knots were unremarkable.

As far as the crime scene was concerned, there was nothing of any interest except a small sterling-silver Saint Christopher's medallion on a broken chain that had been found pressed into the grass under the younger man's right shoulder. There were no usable fingerprints on the metal surfaces. The medallion itself was not mass produced, but seemed to be quite old. On the edge of the Polaroid photo enclosed with the report, Liz had added in her scrawling handwriting, *Family heirloom?*

Carol made a note to ask if either Bucci or Bayliss had worn a Saint Christopher's medallion, realizing as she did so that it could have been lost by someone else long before the bodies were deposited on the grass.

She would have a report from ballistics shortly,

but it was already obvious from the range of bullets taken from the bodies during the autopsies that a variety of firearms had been used. Carol had a bizarre picture of firing squad members discussing muzzle velocity and the properties of ammunition as each selected a favorite weapon, then standing in a group to aim and fire at two blindfolded victims. Had it happened inside a barn? Or had Bayliss and Bucci felt the sun on their faces before they died?

"People way higher up on the ASIO food chain than me are dealing with your Commissioner and the necessary pollies," said Denise Cleveer with the exuberant good humor Carol always associated with her. "But they trust me to brief you personally, since it looks like we'll be working together."

Feeling like some clandestine character in a spy novel, Carol had followed instructions and made a circuitous way to the Circular Quay office building where Denise Cleever was waiting for her.

Now, seated in a bland room with a beguiling view of Sydney Harbour, Carol looked at Denise assessingly. The ASIO agent had lost weight, her honey-blonde hair was longer, and she wore glasses with tortoiseshell frames. Carol was used to seeing her casually dressed, but today Denise had on a dark blue suit fully as tailored as Carol's own.

Denise smiled at Carol's examination. "The specs? I got tired of fiddling with contact lens. Besides, I think it gives me a serious air." Her smile broadened. "And I'm dressing for success. The woman you see before you is promotion material."

Nodding gravely, Carol said, "I've never doubted it."

"How about you, Carol? Chief Inspector Carol Ashton sounds good to me. Or Superintendent Ashton. *That* really has a ring to it, and a promotion's long overdue."

Carol made a face at her. "Don't hold your breath. Besides, it would give me even more paperwork than I've got already."

There was a slim black folder on the desk in front of Denise. She flicked it open. "This case won't add much to the paper wars — anything written will be on a strict need-to-know basis, and most of it will be classified."

"Just getting here to this office made me feel like a secondhand spy," said Carol, thinking of precautions she had been told to take to get to the building.

"Never secondhand," grinned Denise. "And you have no idea how elaborate we can get if we seriously thought you were under surveillance."

Carol felt a tinge of excitement, of unease. "Under surveillance by whom?"

"A group we've been aware of for some time." Denise settled back in her chair. "Very shadowy, we don't have much more than a few disturbing whispers, a vaguely suspicious death, and a name — Inner Circle."

"A suspicious death?"

"Yes, an environmentalist — Neal Rudin. He was a local activist who lived in the district." She took a photograph from the folder and passed it over to Carol. "He was asking a lot of uncomfortable questions about what was happening to protected species, most particularly a koala colony, on land belonging to a long-established local family by the double-barreled name of Cosil-Ross. Made himself very unpopular with the locals, but there'd just been a bit of name-calling, no threats. Then Rudin was killed in a shooting accident."

The black-and-white photo showed a youngish man in hiking gear shading his eyes with one hand as he squinted into the sun. Carol said, "An environmentalist with a gun? Isn't that contradictory?"

"Not living targets, Carol — clay pigeons. Rudin was a skeet shooter, and very good at it. For some reason he climbed through a barbed-wire fence with a loaded shotgun and it went off, killing him instantly. It looked like an accident. There certainly wasn't anything to point to murder, but we were suspicious because the landowners he was at odds with just happen to be on our list of possible Inner Circle members. That made it clear we had to put an agent there on the ground."

"Wayne Bucci."

Denise looked grim. "That's not his real name, but I'll call him that. He'd been in place for a couple of months, working as a part-time mechanic at the local garage. He drank at the pub, got caught up in the local comings and goings, and generally socialized with as wide a range of people as possible. He was sure he was getting closer to the underground cell. Wayne didn't think anyone suspected he was anything but what he seemed. When he had what seemed to be a receptive audience he said all the right things about conspiracies and the government, and he let drop that he was an expert with explosives — which he was, of course. We knew that they'd gone to the trouble of checking his background and it had held up, so we were reasonably certain that he was going to be recruited."

"Could you check to see if he wore an antique silver Saint Christopher medallion? One was found at the crime scene."

"I can tell you now, Wayne wouldn't have had anything like that, because it wouldn't fit in with the personality of the person he was playing."

Carol tried to imagine what it would be like to play a role, knowing that one slip might mean discovery and possible death. She said, "Was there anything interesting in his last report?"

Denise sighed. "When he called in, Wayne was gung ho about the whole situation. He said it had been arranged for him to meet with militia members the next day. Wayne hadn't been given any names, but the guy who was taking him, Rick Turner, has an interesting link to the Cosil-Ross family I mentioned before — his sister is married to one of them."

Denise took off her glasses and rubbed the bridge of her nose. "I trained with him . . . Still can't believe he's dead."

If she closed her eyes, Carol knew she could bring back in vivid detail the morning's autopsies — every sight, every smell held in the stark room. She said, "You know time of death is notoriously difficult to estimate accurately, so all the pathologist will say at this point is that both Wayne and Dean Bayliss died on Sunday."

Replacing her glasses, Denise said, "Wayne was scheduled to make contact last Thursday, but when his controller didn't hear from him there wasn't a big panic. We knew it was possible he was out in the bush somewhere involved in one of those quasi-military maneuvers these groups love to do." Anxiety washed across her face. "I hope to hell he didn't talk. He wasn't tortured, was he?"

"There's no sign of it, unless the volley of shots to his chest destroyed the evidence." Carol had a flash of the lacerated skin on the corpses' wrists and ankles. "They were tied up for some time before they were killed, and both struggled violently to get free. That's torture of a sort."

Denise was silent for a moment, then she said abruptly, "We've got another agent on the ground in Katamulla. We'll pull her out if there's any suggestion her cover's blown."

"She?"

Denise looked at her soberly. "A teacher. She transferred to the local high school at the beginning of the term. Her background's impeccable — she *was* a teacher before she decided to walk on the wild side and join ASIO."

"Walk on the wild side? Is that what you call it?"

Denise had to smile. "Too true. Teaching kids these days seems a lot wilder than anything our organization can dish out."

"Has this teacher heard anything?"

"Not a lot yet, but Agar's son goes to the school and Dean Bayliss is an ex-pupil. You and I will have a debriefing session with her as soon as possible."

Agar's name caught Carol's attention. "Kent Agar. Have you got anything on him?"

"You wish," Denise laughed. "He really is something else, isn't he?"

"I was rather hoping he'd compromised national security, or something like that."

Her light tone obviously didn't disguise her animosity, because Denise gave her a warmly sympathetic smile. "The bastard's been making life hard for you, hasn't he?"

"Hard enough. I think there's a fair chance I'll be taken off this case because of supposed bias on my part."

"No way," said Denise complacently. "My boss has already spoken to the Commissioner. You're on the case. Of course, no one is to know you are in any way linked to ASIO. On the surface it has to look like a standard police investigation."

It was the faces that stayed so close to the surface of Carol's mind: Wayne Bucci, his blind stare somehow defiant; Dean Bayliss slackly gaping at death. "Was Bayliss mentioned in any of Bucci's reports?"

"No, but they would have met." Denise tilted her head. "What do you know about country towns?"

"Not much. I was brought up in Sydney. I did spend most of my holidays with my aunt and uncle in the Blue Mountains. That's the closest I came to the country life."

This brought a derisive snort from Denise. "Blue Mountains? Heck, that's tourist territory."

Recalling an article in last Saturday's *Herald* that extolled Katamulla's Bushranger Week with a dizzy range of activities for visitors, Carol said, "And Katamulla isn't after the tourist dollar? They've elevated some second-rate bushranger to hero status."

Amused, Denise said, "So they have a very active Progress Association."

Katamulla had been fortunate enough to have been the scene of a nineteenth-century shootout between a middling famous bushranger and state troopers. Though not nearly as dramatic as the mythic confrontation in Glenrowan between the infamous Ned Kelly in his homemade armor and the forces of law and order, the Katamulla district's Doom O'Reilly was in the process of being inflated to legendary stature. The Progress Association had declared an entire celebratory week, complete with an elaborate enactment of O'Reilly's ambush and death.

"Since you haven't experienced *real* country living," said Denise, "you need to know that the school in a place like Katamulla is a big deal. It will draw kids from the entire district, and the principal and teachers have a lot more clout in local affairs than they would in a large city. Hell, through the kids the teaching staff probably have links to almost every family in the area."

"Sounds like you're speaking from personal experience."

"Can't you hear the rustic drawl in my voice? My family lived outside Parkes. I'm just a country girl at heart."

To Carol, Denise seemed the antithesis of the image the mention of anything rural created in her mind. Country was slower, safer, attuned to the lazy loop of seasons. Denise, underneath her good-humored persona, was sharp, driven.

Denise went on, "Any small town like Katamulla has pretty well the same social setup. Top of the tree will be the families whose forebears, they'll tell you in numbing detail, originally settled the district. The local churches and the clergy will figure fairly largely, as will any established businesses who have been there for years. As I said, the school will be important and the principal, if he or she has been there for some time, will have quite a say in local affairs. I'm having a briefing file prepared for you right now on the specifics of Katamulla, and it'll be ready before you leave here this afternoon." She put up a warning hand. "Carol, don't think this is paranoid, but there's a good possibility your hotel room will be searched. I'm having the information condensed and printed on the lightest weight paper possible so it will be easy to keep with you." Denise's solemn face was suddenly split by a grin. "You might enjoy reading it — Katamulla's got some real characters."

Carol considered what she knew of the place. It was the generic country town, a place you drove through on your way to somewhere else. She remembered she'd stopped there once with Sybil, wandering through the antique shops with their self-consciously rustic wares, having lunch at the pub, which proudly proclaimed its history as a major stop for the stagecoach line.

"Katamulla's pretty small — so *two* undercover agents?"

"Two isn't enough, Carol." Denise stood, and began to move restlessly around the room. "Forgive the lecture, but you need some background. Since the crackdown in the States after the bombing of the federal building in Oklahoma City there's been a move, which has been imitated here, to have extremist militia groups develop a strategy they call 'leaderless resistance'. They go underground in small, secret cells that operate independently of each other to make it harder for law enforcement to detect and infiltrate them."

"You think Inner Circle is one?"

She jabbed an emphatic finger at Carol. "Too right I do! Get this straight — these aren't men playing little boys with toy guns — they're violent groups, well armed and capable of planning and carrying out acts of domestic terrorism. They have a virulent hatred for people who aren't white, right-wing, and heterosexual. Anyone Jewish, in favor of gun control or abortion rights, or any other progressive idea, is seen as a danger to their vision of their perfect world."

She seemed to read doubt in Carol's expression. "Not convinced that Australia could be involved? ASIO has been liaising with the CIA over national security and terrorism. Frankly, it's become all too clear that the federal governments of both the United States and Australia are poorly equipped to handle chemical or biological attacks by terrorists, especially when the threat comes from within. The New York Trade Center and the Oklahoma City bombings were big wake-up calls, and the nerve gas strikes in the Tokyo subway system only emphasized how easy it is for a small group to obtain the money and expertise to develop weapons that will spread panic and destruction."

"And this Inner Circle group is a threat of that order?" Carol knew her skepticism came from her unwillingness to accept the idea that a sleepy little country town in New South Wales could be linked to international terrorism. "In *Katamulla,* of all places?"

"In Katamulla. And other perfectly innocuous places," said Denise firmly. "We've traced the international links between America and Australia. If you know where to look on the Internet you'll be astonished, and alarmed, at the material that's being exchanged. And that's for public consumption — what's being communicated secretly is anyone's worst nightmare. What do you know about the militia movement in the States?"

"No more than most people. They take the Ruby Ridge standoff and the siege at Waco as examples of the federal government gone mad, and believe an armed citizenship is the only way to safeguard personal freedoms."

Denise gestured widely. "Just sit back and let me give you a quick overview. The CIA identifies three major antigovernment categories, although they very often overlap. First are the extreme patriot groups, where white supremacists and anti-Semites are very comfortable. They share a common belief that the federal government is determined to disarm all citizens in preparation for a takeover by a clandestine global force called, they believe, One World Government. It sounds ludicrous, but the patriot groups declare that the United Nations is a front for this secret organization."

Carol found herself wanting to believe this was only an American phenomenon. "Sure, we have neo-Nazis in Australia, but they're inadequate thugs who get some sort of warped sense of identity out of belonging to a group most of society loathes."

"These patriot organizations are a big step up from those yobbos and skinheads," said Denise impatiently, "though they may sometimes manipulate them for muscle. And don't think Australia's escaped the Yanks' problems. ASIO's tracking several dangerous groups that are well financed and well organized and have enough discipline in the ranks to maintain secrecy."

"And they mirror the movement in America?"

"Absolutely." Denise couldn't keep still. She strode over to the window, glanced outside, then swung around to Carol again. "The CIA's second category has its counterpart here too. These are the people who love running about engaging in paramilitary and survival training in preparation for what they believe is an inevitable confrontation with the federal government. According to them, a cabal of all-powerful Jewish bankers is, even as we speak, deliberately undermining the economy so Australia will fall into their hands."

Carol shook her head. "This is serious Looney Tunes."

"You'll love the third bunch of paranoiacs, then," said Denise. "This lot think they can override the entire justice system. They set up their own common-law courts, conduct their own trials, and sentence people in absentia. Their targets are usually prose-cutors, judges, and other government officials. And, of course, they claim to have the right to carry out whatever punishment they decide is appropriate — and it's often a death sentence."

"But this isn't exactly new," said Carol, playing devil's advocate. "There have been kangaroo courts in Australia since early settlement."

"These are a lot more than kangaroo courts. Attempts have been made to intimidate federal judges by announcing that they've been found guilty of various crimes by a so-called people's court and will be sentenced accordingly."

"I gather none has been carried out?"

"In the States these groups often try nuisance tactics, for example, using local and state laws to tie up a person's property with spurious claims that may take months to resolve. Here in Australia we have one federal judge under twenty-four-hour surveillance because of a death sentence passed by one of these people's courts for imaginary crimes, and several other judges have had their security beefed up."

"This must be the lunatic fringe — a few who have personal axes to grind."

Denise stretched. "Dream on, Carol. You might find it hard to believe, but after the Oklahoma City bombing killed hundreds of innocent people, the numbers joining militias in the States just exploded. Now there are at least eight hundred patriot groups, armed to the teeth, and paranoid about any government authority. Of those, about a hundred and forty are regarded as extremist — so extremist that they swear the United States government deliberately bombed their own federal building in Oklahoma so they could have a justification to crack down on the whole militia movement."

"And how extreme is Inner Circle?"

Denise shrugged. "Judging from our intelligence, Inner Circle has the potential to be right up there with the worst of them. We were alerted of the existence of the group by the FBI, and since then we've picked up clues from shortwave transmissions and coded references on the Internet. In fact, the encryption software they use is incredibly sophisticated."

Carol spread her hands. "I just find it hard to believe that there's enough hatred and fear against the Australian government to fuel this kind of concentrated terrorism."

"Believe it," said Denise with a grim smile. "One reason we're focusing on Inner Circle is that we have information that it's the key cell of an organization that has covert militia groups in other parts of the country — two in Victoria, two additional ones in northern New South Wales, and five in Queensland. Our run-of-the-mill homegrown militia groups think it's bad enough that Australia has never allowed handguns in private hands, but the crackdown on semiautomatic rifles and shotguns after the Tasmanian massacre convinced them that there's a government policy to prevent citizens from lawfully owning arms. The extremist groups go a step further: They're positive that it's a full-blown government conspiracy, so they've been stockpiling everything they can get their hands on and also illegally importing guns, particularly from the United States."

"Hell," said Carol with mock concern, "I'll be outgunned."

"Not so!" Denise was suddenly energized and laughing. "Eat your heart out, James Bond! Come down to the basement and see what we've got in personal protection and surveillance. There's the latest in concealed holsters, and wait until you see the gorgeous little subcompact Glock semiautomatics."

At the doorway she paused. "I didn't mention, did I, that our intelligence is that Inner Circle is led by a woman?"

"A woman?" Carol added sardonically, "Can Inner Circle be all *that* bad, then?"

"I'd say. I always like to think the female is deadlier than the male. It's a feminist thing..."

CHAPTER FIVE

Kent Agar had reluctantly agreed to see Carol and Bourke in the late afternoon. "Parliament is sitting," he'd snapped on the phone, "so I can only spare you a few minutes."

The interview was not in the Colonial Georgian elegance of State Parliament House in Macquarie Street, but in the modern state government office building concealed behind it. The politician's office was small but well appointed. The large rolltop desk was obviously an antique, as was the oak bookcase filled with leather-bound volumes. Three sleek black chairs and a low glass coffee table formed an island near the window, which had a soothing view of the Domain parkland with its expanses of green grass and brooding Moreton Bay Fig trees.

Agar kept them waiting, eventually rushing through his office door in a petulant rush. "This is bloody inconvenient!"

Yesterday's pale, shaken man had gone, and Agar's whiplash impatience, his usual response to any inconvenience or opposition, had returned. He was dressed as he had been the day before: smart dark-gray double-breasted suit, white shirt, and bright red bow tie.

He flung himself in the third chair, eyeing Bourke, but not acknowledging him. To Carol he said, "Frankly, Inspector, I'm more than surprised you're still on the case." His supercilious eyebrows rose. "I believe it's called conflict of interest."

Carol ignored his sneering comment. "As you must know, Mr. Agar, the body you recognized was definitely identified as Dean Bayliss, a friend of your son's. The local officer hasn't been able to interview him yet, but hopes to do so tomorrow."

He pressed his thin lips together. "So? Scott's just turned eighteen. You don't need my permission."

Bourke flipped a page in his notebook. "When did you last see Dean Bayliss, Mr. Agar?"

"I've no idea."

Bourke's mouth twitched at this flat response. "Last week? A month ago? The day before yesterday?"

Agar's narrow face flushed. "Are you trying to be funny, Sergeant? If so, I suggest you think again."

"Was Bayliss a frequent visitor to your home?" asked Bourke agreeably.

"My son has a lot of friends. I'm a busy man, and I don't pay that much attention." He ostentatiously consulted his watch. "Now, if that's all . . ."

Carol passed over a facial shot of Wayne Bucci taken after the blindfold had been removed at the morgue. Agar took it unwillingly and gave it a cursory glance. "The other body? Never seen him before in my life."

"Are you sure?" asked Bourke. "Check it again."

Flipping the photograph onto the glass coffee table, Agar said acidly, "This is a waste of time. I have to get back to the House."

Carol said mildly, "You spend a lot of time in Katamulla."

"So? My family's lived there for over a hundred and fifty years. It's my home. I spend most of my time there when parliament isn't in session."

Passing him another photograph of Bucci, this one taken when he was alive and smiling, Carol said, "We believe that this man has been living in Katamulla for the past few months. His name was Wayne Bucci. I gather he was quite active socially. There's every chance that you have met him, perhaps at some fund-raising, or at the pub."

Agar didn't look at the photo. "Don't know him." He handed it back. The charge of brittle energy that had propelled him into the room seemed to be dissipating, and his face looked pinched.

"Do you recognize this?" Carol passed Agar the Polaroid of the medallion found at the crime scene.

He glared at it. "What is it? Some cheap jewelry?"

Carol could see the tremor in his fingers. She said, "It's a sterling-silver Saint Christopher."

He shoved it back to her. "Nothing I'd wear."

"You've never seen it before?"

"No."

Bourke showed him an illustration of a Volvo station wagon taken from a used-vehicle catalog. "Do you know anyone who owns this model Volvo, perhaps in dark brown?"

The politician shrugged. "It's a common enough model. Maybe someone I know has one, but I can't think who." His glance sharpened. "Why are you asking?"

"A witness says a vehicle similar to this was outside your residence about the right time for the disposal of the bodies."

"Stolen, no doubt," said Agar crisply.

Carol watched him closely. No vehicle answering the Volvo's description had been reported stolen in the seventy-two hours prior to the discovery of the bodies. Although it was unlikely that the Volvo belonged to one of the murderers, it was certainly the type of vehicle found in a country area. "Perhaps someone in Katamulla or the surrounding district drives a similar Volvo?" she said.

"I've told you I don't recognize it."

Abandoning the subject, Carol said, "Exactly when did you arrive home last night, Mr. Agar?"

"I told you yesterday morning. My driver dropped me off about eleven-thirty. You can check that. And I went straight to bed."

"You were alone?"

Bourke's question ignited Agar's temper. "Of

course I was alone! My wife and son live in Katamulla. I not sure what you're suggesting, Sergeant, but I don't like your tone."

Carol said, "Who has your new address in Burma Drive?"

"Is this really necessary? I don't know... My staff. Friends. Family members."

"Anyone in the media?"

His quick smile was malicious. "*You* know, better than I, how the media get information."

Unsure if he was needling her over her relationship with Madeline, Carol said more tersely than she intended, "Would you answer the question, please. Have you given your address to any outlets?"

"Jesus! I don't keep track of these things. And I can't see why it's of such interest."

Bourke cleared his throat. "It seems very likely the bodies were deliberately placed on your property, Mr. Agar. Perhaps you noticed how they were arranged? We were wondering if it had any significance for you." When Agar didn't reply, Bourke added helpfully, "I have a photograph of the crime scene here, if you'd like to see it, but in essence, you'll remember the bodies were in a *T* shape. That does mean something to you?"

Agar flinched, then said tightly, "Nothing. I can't help you."

These questions were visibly disturbing the politician. He was moving uneasily in his chair, his hands fidgeting first with his bow tie, then the cuffs of his shirt.

Carol leaned forward to deliberately invade his personal space. "So you can think of no one who would do this — perhaps to frighten or warn you?"

He had drawn back almost imperceptibly, but now he visibly rallied, shooting out his hands in an emphatic gesture. "You're asking me if I have any enemies, Inspector?" His voice was full of sarcastic incredulity. "Only every bleeding-heart environmentalist, every wild-eyed do-gooder. You can make up the list yourself. Add anyone who's attacked me for my pro-life, pro-family views. I think you'll find that will keep you occupied for some time."

Agar got to his feet. "I must go. I trust you can see yourselves out of the building."

Waiting for the lift, Bourke said to Carol, "He knows who did it . . . And he's scared shitless."

Carol raised an astonished eyebrow when she found the preliminary post-mortem reports waiting on her desk. This was lightning speed — even for very urgent cases several days was the norm — and obviously had been prompted by instructions from the very top. As she went to get a mug of close-to-undrinkable police coffee, she wondered if the Commissioner would speak with her himself. Denise had said that ASIO was requesting that Carol stay on the case and liaise with a field officer, meaning, of course, Denise herself. Carol had pointed out that since Mark Bourke was involved in the investigation, he had to be briefed, and this was awaiting clearance in the security organization's hierarchy.

She chatted for a few moments with a couple of colleagues in the cramped little kitchen alcove, listened to a bawdy story that featured Kent Agar and two dead bodies — Carol always found it remarkable how fast jokes were generated by newsworthy events — and then made her way back to her office.

Sipping the black coffee, she skimmed through the preliminary post-mortems. The reports didn't add much to what Carol had learned at the morgue, although the blood tests were back, indicating that both Bucci and Bayliss had low levels of alcohol in their systems. Neither had eaten a meal recently as both stomachs were empty. The two men had been healthy, although Bucci had signs of early atherosclerosis. Death in each case had been from firearms, the massive trauma to the chest and contents virtually shredding the heart and lungs. Dr. Duke estimated that they had died at approximately the same time, but since they had been shot elsewhere then moved sometime after death, and there was no evidence to show where their bodies had been stored before being dumped, it was impossible to come up with narrow parameters for time of death.

Carol knew that rigor mortis began at five to seven hours, the progressive stiffening taking a set pattern that began in the corpse's face then spread progressively to the neck, shoulders, arms, abdomen, and legs. Fully established at twelve to eighteen hours, the rigidity would last for about twelve hours, then fade in the same sequence.

However, the temperature in the environment was a complicating factor — stiffening was accelerated by heat, delayed by cold — as was a struggle by the victim before death, which often had the effect of speeding the onset of rigor.

Bucci and Bayliss had been discovered just before six on Monday morning, and the police doctor, arriving an hour later, observed that rigor was complete. At the morgue, it had been noted that rigor mortis had completely gone by late Monday afternoon. Working back from this disappearance of rigor, and taking into account possible variables, Dr. Duke had calculated that each death had occurred somewhere between twenty-four and thirty-six hours previously, a twelve-hour window of time that stretched from early Sunday morning to the afternoon of the same day.

Normally time of death could be narrowed by evidence that a victim was alive at a certain time, but so far no one had come forward to say that they had seen Bucci after Thursday, and Dean Bayliss had taken the weekend off from his bakery job and had not been seen since Friday afternoon.

She examined the body diagrams that indicated the pattern of gunshots the two victims had sustained. Individual outlines were printed in stark black lines for the front, back, and each side of the body, and on these the pathologist had marked each wound. Where clarification was necessary, an arrow led to a brief written note.

The diagrams showed Bayliss and Bucci had had a similar pattern of injuries, with the majority to the chest area. A smaller number of outlet wounds on the back showed that some projectiles had burst completely through the barrier of flesh and bone.

As she examined the diagrams of Wayne Bucci's cataclysmic wounds, Bourke came into her office. "Mark, the very man I wanted to see. I've got the prelim on the posts here from Jeff Duke." She handed him the pages. "This has got to be some kind of speed record."

"Put it down to your unconscious, natural charm,"

said Bourke facetiously. "You know Duke will do anything for you."

He perched himself on the plain wooden chair that faced her desk. "I went to see ballistics," he said, "since I knew even your charisma has limits. As it was, I had to make a pest of myself until I finally got some information."

"They only got the evidence this morning, Mark."

"Maybe, but someone's given them the hurry-up, because they were hard at work." He pulled thoughtfully at his ear. "A collection of firearms were used, with a wide range of calibers from twenty-two upward. The same with the ammunition, which, apart from the standard stuff, included XTP bullets that expand on impact to cause the maximum tissue damage."

"Evidently a real little homegrown battalion," said Carol with a grimace. "Any estimation of how many different guns were used?"

"What complicates it is the fragmentation of some of the bullets, plus the ones that went right through the bodies. As well, we don't know how many were crash-hot shots. Some might have missed entirely. The best guess is five, maybe six, and probably a mixture of handguns and rifles."

"The same weapons killed both victims?"

"Seems that way, and I can tell you the bloke with the twenty-two is a lousy shot," said Bourke with sour amusement, "since ballistics says it was the same person who hit Bayliss in the shoulder and Bucci in the lower abdomen."

Carol's phone began to ring insistently. She glared at the receiver, then snatched it up. "Carol Ashton." She listened for a long moment, then said, "I've no comment to make at this time..." As soon as she put down the phone, it rang again. Putting her hand on the receiver, she said to Bourke, "Someone at the morgue's leaked info about the post-mortems this morning. Every journalist in town will be ringing asking for confirmation."

He went to the door of her office. "If you piss that call off, Carol, I'll get any others intercepted and rerouted to police PR. Can't imagine why they didn't go there first, anyway."

Picking up the receiver, Carol muffled it with her hand as she said to Bourke, "That first call — the reporter said that she'd been told by the usual anonymous source of course — that I've got specific information that will embarrass the state government. That's why they're calling me direct."

"Someone has it in for you, do you think?"

"Or the government," said Carol.

The Commissioner had a written message delivered to her by hand. She was to be in his office at nine that night, and this appointment was to be kept confidential. The pile of papers in her in-tray convinced Carol that she had enough to keep her busy until then.

She called her Aunt Sarah in the Blue Mountains and cajoled her into coming down to Sydney to look after the house and cats for a few days, then dialed Madeline's private line at the channel, hoping to catch her before she went to makeup.

"Carol!" said Madeline, delighted. "I'm just on my way out the door. You'd better be calling to make a definite date. I'll chat up Kent Agar to soothe him after I grill him on the show, then I'll be free."

"I'm sorry, it'll have to be later in the week."

"Tomorrow night's not possible. What's wrong with tonight?" Madeline sounded aggrieved. "It doesn't matter what time it is. I'll get Edna to leave something out for a late supper."

Carol could imagine Madeline standing by her desk in her elegant office with its deep-pile navy carpet and expensive leather couches, looking just as sleek and unassailable as her furnishings.

"I'll take a rain check on tonight," said Carol. "And I have a compelling reason. The cats. I've been out so often lately that Jeffrey and Sinker treat me like a stranger in my own house. Jenny from next door feeds them, but they've started to look at me with such contemptuous scorn that I really think I have to do something to win back their feline good favor."

"So the cats come first," said Madeline, disgusted. A pause, then Madeline added in the tone of a casual afterthought, "Are you planning to go to Katamulla yourself?"

"Possibly."

Her cautious tone amused Madeline. "I'm not trying to worm classified information out of you, Carol. I may be there myself in the next day or so. I've got staff down there setting up interviews. If the story has legs, I'll go down myself."

Carol felt a twinge of sympathy for those country people who had some connection with the victims, especially the relatives of Dean Bayliss. The local investigation was still in the hands of Sergeant Griffin and his constable, so she imagined any questions would be considerately phrased. This wasn't likely to be the case with reporters trained to go for the jugular.

"By the way . . ." Madeline sounded offhand, ". . . I was wondering if you'd like to fill me in a little about the autopsies."

"What've you heard?"

"Don't snap at me, Carol. I've got the same as everyone else. The two victims were tied up, blindfolded, had yellow targets pinned to their chests, and were then executed. And the amateur firing squad used a variety of weapons."

"I suppose it's hopeless to ask you for your source?"

"Hopeless," said Madeline cheerfully. "You know I'd never get another scoop if I named names." Virtuous, she added, "And there's the ethical question, of course."

"If I run a name by you, perhaps you might comment."

"Unlikely, darling."

Thinking of the inquisitive manner of the young doctor at the morgue, Carol said, "Price. Dr. Jeanine Price." When there was no reply, Carol added persuasively, "Am I warm? Madeline, I really need to know."

After a moment Madeline said conversationally, "Unseasonably hot for this time of year, isn't it?"

Bourke had rushed off to catch a reception at the Art Gallery of New South Wales, where his wife, Pat James, was involved in the first public showing of

Internet Screams, a work by a very controversial Czech artist. Protests were expected, as the several million dollars the painting had cost had stirred outrage in some quarters. The week before, Kent Agar had seized the opportunity to condemn the work as "vomit on canvas," thundering indignant questions in state parliament about the acquisition policies of the Gallery and the abuse of taxpayers' hard-earned money.

As Carol put a note on Bourke's desk to ask him to check out Jeanine Price as the source of leaks from the morgue, she thought affectionately of Pat, whose no-nonsense, resilient nature and robust figure were at odds with Carol's preconceptions of what someone artistic should be like.

"The Shipley Report" began at seven. Carol went back to her office, passing up another mug of coffee — the caffeine jolt would help, but the taste became more vile as the day went on — and turned on the television set to see her own face on the screen. Channel Thirteen's news program was just ending, and the double murder was featured in the summary of major news stories. Carol saw herself on the steps talking to Agar and then, in a later shot, turning away from the cameras as the reporter who had invaded the cordon shouted a question. ". . . Inspector Carol Ashton is no stranger to controversy," the voice-over confided, "and this mysterious double execution may have links both to organized crime *and* the New South Wales government!" There was a shot of the gurneys wheeling the bodies away from the crime scene. "Further exclusive details at eleven . . ."

Madeline Shipley began her news magazine show

with a plug for viewers to keep tuned for an exclusive live interview with Kent Agar. She smiled serenely from the screen as she described him, ". . . the prominent, crusading politician who to some is a rabid right-winger, to others the savior of the family values that have made our country great."

"Give me a break!" Carol said to herself.

She worked steadily through a pile of paperwork, glancing up every now and then to check the screen. "The Shipley Report" had its usual parade of items: a million-dollar lottery winner who was refusing to share the prize with coworkers who claimed to have contributed to the ticket; a runaway united with her sobbing mother; a scare warning about pesticide residue in fruit and vegetables; the requisite sad/happy animal story, in this case an abandoned puppy being rescued from a storm water drain.

". . . And now, in a 'Shipley Report' exclusive, we speak with a politician both praised and reviled and who now is touched by the horror of multiple murder!"

Carol put down her gold pen and leaned back to watch. A quick montage of scenes successively depicted police crime-scene tape flapping in a breeze, the screens hiding the bodies, a pan to Agar's house with the politician himself opening the door and walking down the steps to be met by Carol, the loaded gurneys trundling by and, finally, a close-up of a headline from a newspaper, POLICE SOFT ON CRIME AGAR STATES.

Madeline was low-key, serious, as she introduced Agar. He was dressed as Carol had seen him that afternoon.

"Madeline," he said gravely, sincerely, "I don't

think I speak too strongly when I say the very foundations of our society are threatened by these random deaths." He put up a hand, as if to forestall her interruption. "I say to you, when a member of parliament can be touched by the hand of organized crime — by the violence that inevitably accompanies the loathsome trade in prostitution and drugs — then no one, *no one* is safe!"

He stared straight into the camera. "And the Police Service," he intoned, "have had every opportunity to cut out the cancer that afflicts our state. To put away the Mr. Bigs of organized crime. *Every* opportunity!"

He threw back his head and his haughty eyebrows rose. "Why hasn't this happened? Because I believe there is corruption in the very people sworn to protect us and our families!"

"Give me a break," said Carol for the second time.

CHAPTER SIX

The Commissioner's office was luxurious in an uncompromisingly masculine way. The thick carpet muffled footsteps, the furniture was dark and heavy, with no concession to frivolous ornamentation — everything in the room was intended to be strictly functional. There were no curtains at the windows, which looked out at the lights of the city. Somewhere, far below, a siren wailed in the street.

Carol reflected that the Commissioner, with his hulking body, booming voice, and awkward gestures, never seemed entirely comfortable in these surroundings. In contrast, the other man in the office, a stranger to her, seemed very much at ease. Carol assessed him as he rose smoothly to shake hands.

He was short, dapper, and had a silky quality about him, a facile glossiness that was reinforced by his light, somehow insinuating voice. "Inspector Ashton. I'm so pleased to meet you. My name is Malcolm Trevorwill. I'm with ASIO, as you might suspect."

His handshake was firm and brief; his quick smile flickered, then disappeared.

The Commissioner waved Carol to a chair. "You've been briefed by Agent Cleever, I understand," he rumbled.

"Yes. This afternoon."

"Then you already have some idea of the gravity of the situation," said Malcolm Trevorwill. He took papers from a slim briefcase on the floor by his seat. "Inspector, these are classified documents. I ask you to read them here and now. You may ask questions, but you may not take notes. I'm sure you realize that you may not discuss any of the contents with anyone but authorized personnel."

As Trevorwill passed the stapled pages to Carol, the Commissioner cleared his throat. "Coffee?" He indicated an insulated carafe that sat on a tray with three cups and a plate of shortbread.

"Thank you. Black." Carol was secure in the knowledge that this executive brew would be far superior to the coffee she usually drank at work.

The room became silent, the only noise the coffee splashing into cups, then the delicate click as Trevorwill stirred in sugar. Carol swiftly scanned the

four double-spaced pages and the single-spaced adden-
dum, then went back to the beginning and reread the
pages with slow concentration.

She looked up. "There's no direct evidence that
the sarin has gone to the Inner Circle group?"

Trevorwill took a delicate swallow, then put down
his cup on the saucer. His glance included both Carol
and the Commissioner as he answered, "No direct
evidence, but it's an excellent educated guess. We
only heard about the nerve gas shipment after the
fact and traced its route by sea from Los Angeles to
Sydney. Coded communications we've been able to
intercept associate the shipment to a secret militia
group. On the Internet, a yellow or gold circle has
been used as a secret signal to identify this group,
and our agent on the ground confirmed that he'd
heard this symbol associated with a covert organization calling itself Inner Circle and located in the
Katamulla area."

After her meeting with Denise, Carol had checked
a large-scale map of New South Wales. "There are
several townships in the district," she said. "Why
Katamulla in particular?"

"Bushwalkers came across a dump of dead cattle
in a gully off a little-used track in Boolworrie
National Park, which is near Katamulla. We were
alerted when the park authorities decided the animals
had died from something extraordinary. Our
technicians determined it was sarin."

Carol had already known that sarin was the nerve
gas used by the Japanese religious cult Aum Supreme
Truth in the subway attacks that had killed twelve
and sickened hundreds, but until she had read the

report Trevorwill had given her, she had not appreciated how deadly the substance was in a restricted space, or that it was so readily available.

"The sarin disappeared from a U.S. Army depot in Utah where it was stored with mustard gas and other chemical weapons preparatory to destruction in a high-temperature incinerator," said Trevorwill. "This is the first of eight such incinerators being constructed over the next ten years or so, each costing over a billion to build and operate. The stockpiling of the projectiles and bombs holding these substances at each site will provide extremist groups with tempting targets to hit." He gave a bleak smile. "In this particular case, it could have been worse — the Utah site also has supplies of VX, the deadliest nerve agent in the U.S. arsenal."

Sarin seemed quite deadly enough to Carol. The document she held summarized the effects of the nerve gas succinctly. Victims' muscles would twitch, saliva would foam, lungs would constrict and fill with fluid. Suffocation rapidly followed. Those fortunate enough to be exposed to lower concentrations would be immobilized by watering eyes and stomach cramps. All personnel likely to be exposed to sarin should carry gas masks and a nerve gas antidote syringe.

"The American end," said the Commissioner. "Surely there's some joy there? Names? Hard information about who was getting the stuff in Australia?"

Trevorwill shook his head. "They're as slippery as eels. The FBI's been monitoring the group, who call themselves Complete Freedom Militia, for some time. There have been stories that they planned to contaminate the Seattle water supply with anthrax, but no hard evidence. The theft of the sarin looks like an inside job, but it was linked to this particular militia because two members just happened to be in the general area of the Utah Army Depot at the time. But again, there's no hard evidence."

"Anthrax?" said the Commissioner sharply. "Do you think this Inner Circle crowd have biological weapons too?"

"It's always a possibility." Trevorwill reached over and took the pages from Carol. "We can hope not, since a biological attack from a virulent bacillus like anthrax could put hundreds of thousands at risk. At least sarin dilutes quickly in air, so effective use requires an enclosed space."

Jutting his jaw, the Commissioner said, "This is bloody serious."

"Indeed." Trevorwill raised his eyebrows fractionally to Carol, "You can see, Inspector, why we need your total cooperation with regard to this matter."

"Of course you have Inspector Ashton's cooperation," said the Commissioner. He made a wide, all-inclusive gesture. "*And* you have all the resources of the entire New South Wales Police Service available to you."

Trevorwill seemed unimpressed. "It's vital that we keep total security regarding this matter. Acknowledging that, the Federal Police have agreed to remain on the sidelines for the moment. Basically, ASIO has only a few facts, suppositions, and names to play with. Until the key Inner Circle players are identified, we can't make any move that will alert the group. If we do, they'll melt away and any evidence will be destroyed or concealed. Then they'll spring up somewhere else."

He inclined his head toward Carol. "But Inspector Ashton has every reason to go to Katamulla and ask searching questions. She is investigating a double murder, and no one will be surprised to find her inquiring closely into Wayne Bucci's movements and that of his associates."

Carol said, "Denise Cleever told me this afternoon that your agent reported that a local man, Rick Turner, was to take him to meet the Inner Circle leaders. I'll have to find someone else to tell me they were together before I can question him, otherwise he, and others involved, will be tipped off that I have some unusual sources of information."

"Exactly. I see you appreciate the delicacy of the situation." He glanced over at the Commissioner. "Before you arrived, Inspector, we were discussing certain logistics . . ."

The Commissioner responded on cue. "The media have already been told that we're pursuing lines of inquiry that indicate that the murders are linked to a drug deal gone wrong. It's not as if that area of the country hasn't been involved in drugs before, so it's a reasonable cover story."

"Does the regional commander know the real situation?"

"I've spoken to Chief Superintendent Healy myself," he said heavily. "He knows the minimum he needs to know — that ASIO's on the ground in his district. Other than that, it's vital that all personnel — and that includes the sergeant and senior constable in Katamulla — are kept in the dark."

"Mark Bourke will be working closely with me."

The leather chair creaked as Trevorwill leaned forward. "Denise Cleever has advised us that Sergeant Bourke has met her before, so in order to explain her presence in Katamulla, it's necessary that he know that ASIO is interested in the militia group. However, Bourke is not to be told anything about the possibility that Inner Circle has sarin, or that this group is the leader of a network of extremist cells."

"You should know that it's likely that Madeline Shipley and a film crew will be in Katamulla too," Carol said. "Although I'm not sure if they ever met, it's possible she may recognize Denise Cleever from the Marla Strickland case."

"That could be a problem." Trevorwill pressed his forefinger against his mouth as he considered the issue. "We're always very reluctant to request a D-notice. An official security blackout always gets the media in a lather, and someone could say something out of line."

He thought for a moment longer, then leaned back to regard Carol. "Madeline Shipley is a personal friend of yours, isn't she?"

Carol wondered if her file indicated *how* personal. "I know her, yes."

"If it appears that Shipley will definitely be in the area, I'll arrange for her to be advised there's a covert operation in place, but that's all she'll know. Apart from that, I'll leave it to you and Agent Cleever to assess the situation and take appropriate steps on a personal level."

His lips quirked. "Has Denise Cleever mentioned her undercover role? Under the name of Denise North, she's a representative for educational and general publishers who's in the area to make contacts and drum up book orders."

The Commissioner checked his watch. "I have a meeting . . ."

"We're finished, I think," said Trevorwill. "Any further questions you have, Inspector, you can direct to Agent Cleever. She'll approach you first, probably at the Katamulla Hotel, where you'll both be staying."

"Carol, when you get there tomorrow," said the Commissioner with a grin, "be sure to put yourself up in the best room the pub can offer. I'll make sure all your expenses are authorized."

Carol had had experience of accommodation in small country town pubs before. "Thanks," she said without noticeable gratitude.

CHAPTER SEVEN

Driving down to Katamulla, Carol wore a tailored navy pantsuit to hide the pocket-size subcompact Glock 27 she was wearing in an ankle holster. Under her jacket in a polymer nylon shoulder holster she had a nine-millimeter Beretta, its weight under her left arm reassuring.

This morning when she'd dressed after her run she'd felt faintly ridiculous to be wearing this much firepower, but an early session with a police arms specialist had changed her mind. As she'd fired at the human outlines of the targets at the range, she'd thought of the yellow circles on Bayliss and Bucci's chests. She could imagine their murderers forming a line, their hands caressing the cold metal of their weapons. Were they silent, or did they nervously joke with one another before someone gave them the signal to fire?

Mark Bourke would be coming down later, so she'd left Sydney alone, elated to be on the road. She put on sunglasses against the bright sunlight, turned up the volume on a favorite CD of rock-and-roll classics, and sang along as the city slipped away. Soon she was barreling along the highway in light traffic, whipping past stands of gum trees and rolling paddocks green from unseasonable warmth and rain.

Abruptly, the sun was gone. She took off her sunglasses as the light faded. The sky ahead boiled with purple and gray clouds. Lightning flickered, but any thunder was drowned by the pounding music. Cars coming the other way were wet and had headlights glaring.

She came around a long slow curve and drove into an avalanche of water, the rain falling so heavily that, even at maximum, the wipers couldn't clear the glass. She slowed, turned on the lights and, when it slackened a little, accelerated again. She felt she was in a cocoon whose boundaries were determined by sound: the clack of the wipers, the hiss of tires on the wet road, the healthy hum of the engine, the music pouring from the speakers to surround her.

Carol was lit by a sudden shaft of pure happiness. When, puzzled, she examined it, the feeling faded, although an impression of the emotion lingered like an afterimage.

The rain stopped as she reached the outskirts of

Katamulla. A high wind was shredding the dark clouds so that the sun could break through. The wet road shone in dazzling reflections, and leaves, washed clean, glistened and danced. Turning off the music, Carol put the window down to fill the car with delicious moist scents from the damp earth.

She angle parked her car in the main street, which was full of leisurely activity. Traffic moved more slowly here than in the city, and pedestrians had time to stop and talk. Somehow this place seemed to contain the essence of every country town she remembered from her youth. Sitting in the backseat on family holidays, she would scan each place to locate a milk bar, so she could cajole her parents for an ice cream or double-chocolate malted milk. Katamulla's main street was from that past. To her delight, she saw the Imperial Cafe, complete with etched glass and ancient Formica countertops. Milkshakes were listed, but the ice cream was no longer in deep metal barrels. Brightly colored posters promised explosive taste delights of the variety of prepackaged ice cream treats.

Carol continued to stroll down the street. A wide banner suspended across the road declared BUSH-RANGER WEEK: DOOM O'REILLY CELEBRATIONS. The town hall, solemn in red brick, bore an ornate plaque dedicated to some long-dead local council member. It sat solidly across from the sandstone post office, which sported an odd red spire in a rakish ecclesiastical touch. Dividing the road was a gray granite memorial inscribed with the names of native sons and daughters who had perished in the twentieth century's many wars.

Three churches vied for prominent positions: St.

Luke's was plain and businesslike Anglican, but the notice board outside testified to a certain trendiness — the rock gospel service advertised for Sunday night included a laser light show. On the other side of the street the patron saint of the Catholic Church of St. Francis smiled amiably at the passing traffic from his perch on the facade of a standard-issue building with spire and stained glass windows. Farther along the Uniting Church, St. Clement's, contrasted with a cheerfully ugly box-shaped edifice painted an unbecoming shade of ocher yellow.

Her stomach growled. Breakfast had been her usual toast and coffee hours before, so Carol went back to the Imperial Cafe, which was humming with a lunchtime crowd. The middle-aged waitress, cheery in a pink uniform one size too small, showed Carol to a booth near the back. The imitation leather of the seating was worn but clean, and the speckled Formica table had an island precisely in the center that was made up of industrial-size salt and pepper shakers, two plastic-covered menus, a flip-top glass sugar container, three bottles offering tomato, mustard, and steak sauces, a plastic holder containing paper serviettes in a choice of pink, aqua, or white, and two dispirited artificial roses in a hectic blue vase.

The handwritten menu had delights Carol had forgotten, including savory mince on toast and something she had last ordered in her teens, a mixed grill — steak, sausage, liver, bacon, and a lamb chop all on one plate. Unable to face such a cholesterol challenge, she ordered something marginally healthier, the specialty of the house, an Imperial Hamburger.

While she waited for the food Carol relaxed to let

the conversation and activity flow around her. The country voices were subtly different with a slightly broader, slower cadence. Two men in the booth behind her were discussing grain prices; three young people nearby argued over the relative merits of television stars whose situation comedy they'd watched the night before.

When the waitress delivered the hamburger Carol blinked at its enormous size. The formidable bun was bursting with a thick patty smothered with melted cheese, plus what looked liked every salad ingredient imaginable, including fat slices of purple beetroot. All this was surrounded by huge wedges of potato and chunks of fresh tomato.

"Tea, love?" inquired the waitress.

Even though she knew she couldn't possibly finish this meal as it was, Carol heard herself say, "Double-chocolate malted milkshake, please."

Fortified and feeling distinctly bloated, Carol went back to her car. The waitress, her eyes sharpening with interest, had answered Carol's question about the location of the police station with, "You can't miss it!" and had then proceeded to give complicated instructions that relied on knowledge of local landmarks. Despite her doubts, following these turned out to be reasonably easy, and she found the neat little station with only one wrong turn.

The building had obviously been a residence that had been converted to official use. It stood in the middle of a row of similar small dwellings, each with a carefully tended front garden. But the Katamulla Police Station had a stark white sign announcing its existence, and the front yard had been concreted over to provide a parking area, in the middle of which one skinny gum tree struggled to survive. Close to the worn wooden front steps a dust-streaked car sat in the area designated *Official Vehicles Only.*

Carol walked up the steps, across the bare veranda whose unpainted boards creaked under her weight, and pushed open the front door that had a handprinted sign giving the number to call if the station happened to be unattended.

The hallway inside had been widened by knocking down a wall of a front room. Behind a wooden counter a lanky man in his thirties with a prominent nose and Adam's apple lounged in a chair. He looked up without enthusiasm. "Yeah?"

When Carol identified herself he got quickly to his feet. "Inspector Ashton! We've been expecting you. I'm Senior Constable Kirk. Ken Kirk." He hurried around to her side of the counter, hastily straightening his uniform. "I'm sorry, but Sergeant Griffin is out at the moment, and I'm not sure when he'll be back . . ."

Carol felt a jolt of irritation. She had spoken to Griffin early that morning, and he had indicated he expected to be at the station all afternoon. "I'll take the opportunity to check in at the hotel. Would you mind asking Sergeant Griffin to call me when he gets in? Tell him I'll come back to the station as soon as I hear from him."

Constable Kirk walked her back to her car, assuring her several times that he'd get his sergeant to call the moment he returned. He gave her directions to get back to the main street, instructions that seemed quite different from the ones she had used to get there. After an accidental minitour of the back blocks, she finally found the main artery of the town and parked in front of the Katamulla Hotel, which was freshly painted in tones of cream and deep, dark green.

The wooden two-story building had been restored to something close to its original turn-of-the-century glory. The wide verandas were supported by shaped wooden pillars between which panels featuring the ornate curlicues of cast iron lace extended. Antique advertisements for spirits and beer on mirrored glass were framed on either side of the double entrance doors. A large hand, also imprinted on glass, pointed imperiously left along the veranda, its embellished script declaring, TO BAR.

Inside the main entrance it was darkly hushed and mysterious. Above the broad oak counter a varnished wooden sign indicated that the proprietors were H. AND B. BENNETT, names she recognized from the ASIO briefing file. A door to the left of the counter had a similar sign indicating that it led to the LADIES' BAR, a nod to historical authenticity, although the time had long gone when males and females had been strictly segregated in Australian drinking establishments.

Carol followed the instructions on a card tacked to the top of the counter and rang the small brass bell twice. After a long delay a harried woman with an ugly-attractive face and graying hair escaping from large tortoiseshell combs appeared. "Yes, dear?"

"I have a reservation. In the name of Carol Ashton."

The woman leaned on the counter so that her substantial bosom was supported by her folded arms. "You're the cop from Sydney. I've seen you on the telly. It's about those awful murders, isn't it?"

Carol had a healthy respect for the gossip gathering that could be achieved at a pub — particularly one in a country area. "That's right," she said. "Did you know either of them?"

Carol didn't need to spell out the names. It was a small town, and Dean Bayliss and his family were locals. And she knew Wayne Bucci had been careful to be very sociable, drinking regularly at the pub and striking up conversations at every opportunity.

"Dreadful business," said the woman, shaking her head so that even more wisps of hair escaped from the combs. "Young Dean, I knew him since he was a baby. His father — he's a broken man, you know."

"Beryl, love, I need you in the bar." He was large framed, a strong man gone to seed. "I'll look after things here."

"This is Inspector Ashton, come from Sydney . . ."

He put his hand over the counter and shook Carol's. "Herb Bennett. I'll take you to your room." His face was a long slab, lugubrious and dark jowled. "Got any luggage?"

She followed him up the creaking stairs to the second floor. "Our best room," he said. He put her suitcase down and indicated an inner door. "Bathroom. You don't have to share." He went to open the French doors that led to the wide veranda. A blast of cool, wet air filled the room. "Keep 'em locked when you're out," he said. "Security." He indicated a vinyl folder. "Mealtimes in there. Call if you want anything." Then he was gone.

Carol stood in the middle of the Katamulla Hotel's best room. It was large, with pale yellow floral wallpaper. The polished wooden floor was inadequately covered by a square of fading carpet with a flower pattern. A heavy carved dresser and matching wardrobe took up adjacent walls. The mirrors of both were speckled with age. The black metal-framed double bed had a noticeable dip in the middle of its saffron cotton spread. Carol rolled her eyes, suspecting that it was a genuinely antique mattress.

Crowding a brown clock radio on the bedside table, a canary-colored telephone receiver, in keeping with the yellow theme of the room, sat on a circular cloth of pale lemon. As she regarded it, the phone rang. Constable Kirk was apologetic, but he'd heard from Sergeant Griffin and he wouldn't be available until five-fifteen that afternoon. Would she mind coming to the station then?

Carol said that she'd be there. It wasn't the constable's fault, of course, but she knew her annoyance showed in her voice. She needed an up-to-date briefing about the status of Griffin's inquiries, particularly the interview with Scott, Kent Agar's son, which he had had scheduled for that morning.

Hating to waste time, she stood tapping the receiver with her fingernails, then took out the slim district telephone directory to check the number of the high school.

Katamulla High School was nothing like Carol imagined. She had thought it would be a little ramshackle, but the low-lying spread of buildings had clean modern lines and bright panels of primary colors. Separate from the others, a striking black-and-white building bore in large polished silver letters, COSIL-ROSS HALL. The Cosil-Ross family, she remembered, had substantial landholdings, and, along with the Agars, boasted the longest-established pedigree in the district.

In the driveway Carol slowed her car almost to a stop as a tide of students, released for the day, rushed toward her. The navy blue of their uniforms reinforced the impression of an inexorable river. For one moment Carol had the ridiculous thought that the leaders would reach her car and simply keep walking up and over the top, their feet creating a drumming thunder. She smiled involuntarily as the students automatically divided into two streams and flowed around the vehicle. She looked back and saw that they were reforming into one company as they continued toward the front gate.

The principal, John Webb, had been perfunctory on the phone. He had agreed to see Carol on short notice, but as he had a staff meeting after school, he could only spare her a few minutes. She knew from her briefing file that he had been at Katamulla High for eight years, was married to a preschool teacher who taught in the local kindergarten, and that they had two daughters.

Webb greeted her at the front office where honor rolls on varnished wood listed the names of those students who had contributed notably to the glory of the school. A large tapestry wall hanging was emblazoned with the school crest and motto, TO HIGHER THINGS, in purple and gold. Beside this a substantial plaque noted that this was a gift from the Cosil-Ross family.

Webb's head was too small for his gangling body and, as if to emphasize this, his brown hair was cut very short. The coat of his wrinkled blue suit hung on his narrow sloping shoulders. He had stubby fingers with bitten nails, and he barely brushed palms in his handshake with Carol. "Inspector Ashton, your fame precedes you."

The principal's tone didn't indicate whether he meant this to be ironic, and his flat, expressionless face gave no further clue. He ushered her into a small sitting room adjacent to the general office. It was furnished stylishly with several lounges and matching chairs and had a kitchen alcove with refrigerator and a microwave oven. One whole wall was hung with framed photographs of winning sports teams.

When Carol remarked on the excellent facilities, Webb said, without inflection, "We have benefactors from our local community, and also, Kent Agar's our representative in State Parliament. He supports public education."

"I presume you know Mr. Agar well."

"His son is a student in Year Twelve." His mouth closed on the last word, and Carol could almost imagine she heard his teeth snap together.

"Until last year I believe Dean Bayliss was also a student?"

"Yes." He seemed to think that this might need some elaboration, as, after a pause, he added standard words of regret at the death of a popular, hardworking student. There would, of course, be an official party of pupils and staff at Dean's funeral.

"Was there ever any indication that Dean was involved in anything unlawful?"

"You mean drugs?" A faint flush stained his cheeks. "Absolutely not. I pride myself that Katamulla High has not been infected by such things. I don't pretend that there have never been some problems here, but I have taken immediate, drastic action."

"Not necessarily drugs. Anything."

Webb's lips twitched in a faint smile. "Anything, Inspector? You're casting a wide net there."

Carol tried an air of candor. "We have very little to go on at the moment. His murder was set up as an execution and was possibly meant as a warning. And, as you know, another man was killed with him. There's always a possibility that others may be in danger."

Webb tapped his short fingers on his knee. His hand stilled, as if he'd come to a decision. "I'll introduce you to the staff. We have a meeting in a few minutes, and perhaps you will wish to talk with Dean Bayliss's teachers afterward."

Hiding her surprise at this unexpected cooperation from the principal, Carol followed him down a brightly decorated hallway to a high-ceilinged meeting room full of orange chairs covered in vinyl that were arranged so that five or six each clustered around a circular low table. The hum of conversation abated as Carol and Webb entered, most of the thirty or so people looking with open curiosity at Carol.

The teaching staff was an eclectic group, ranging from some who looked young enough to be students themselves to an ancient man with a straggling white mustache who seemed to be well past retirement age.

Carol wondered which one was Gwen Pickard, the ASIO undercover agent. Several women were in her age group, the early forties.

Webb went to the front of the room and cleared his throat. "Before we begin, I'd like to take the opportunity to introduce Detective Inspector Carol Ashton," he said. "As you all must know, she is here in Katamulla to investigate the murder of Dean Bayliss, a student at the school until last year. She will say a few words now and perhaps, after the meeting, any of you who may have useful information can speak with her personally."

Waiting for the low buzz of reaction to die away, Carol was aware of the mass of the little Glock tugging at her ankle and the considerably heavier Beretta nestling under her left arm. She had practiced drawing from a shoulder holster until the instructor was satisfied. The Glock was a backup, a deadly little semiautomatic pistol that held nine rounds in a magazine and one in the chamber. It could easily be accessed when sitting. She scanned the faces turned toward her. Was there anyone there who had pitilessly watched the two men die?

When the room was silent she spoke briefly, mentioning both Dean Bayliss and Wayne Bucci. ". . . They were murdered together, and at the same time. There must be some link between them, but at this point we have no clear idea what this might be. If any of you has any information, however unimportant or slight it might appear, I would like to speak with you after the staff meeting. If you don't have time then, please give me your name and telephone number and I'll arrange to see you later."

Forty minutes into the meeting — the content of

which seemed fully as boring to the participants as it was to Carol — she checked her watch, then slipped out of the room to find a telephone. She got a recorded message at the police station, so she identified herself, apologized to Sergeant Griffin that she was running late for their five-fifteen appointment, and asked him to wait until she got there.

Back in the staff room, she was relieved to find that things were winding up with the ancient teacher creakily haranguing the group about teacher non-attendance at school drama nights. "I expect better this time, I really do," he snapped, the strands of his straggling mustache seeming to stiffen with indignation. "Is it too much to ask you to miss just *one* night's mindless television to watch the students perform?"

"Too right!" said someone at the back, to general laughter.

Webb stepped quickly to the front to forestall any further discussion. "Now, if there's nothing else . . ." This signal that the meeting was over released a wave of movement and conversation. Raising his voice over the noise, Webb said, "And don't forget Inspector Ashton . . ."

The third person to speak with Carol introduced herself as Gwen Pickard. ". . . This may not be much help, but I did see Dean that Friday before he disappeared. He serves at the bakery, you know."

Carol was fascinated to meet the ASIO operative, knowing that she had given up a teaching career to become, in essence, a spy for her country. Gwen Pickard was, appropriately, quite unremarkable. In her early forties, she had a comfortable body, brown frizzy hair lightly graying, and a web of laughter

92

lines at the corners of her pale blue eyes. Her hands were neat and well manicured, although nicotine stained her fingers.

It had been arranged that the agent volunteer information when she first met Carol, so that there would be every reason for them to be seen speaking with each other. Carol took her name and address and said that she'd be in touch.

At the end of twenty minutes Carol had several leads to follow up. As the last teacher hurried out, John Webb, who had stayed patiently by her side, said, "They can't wait to get away at the end of the day. Can't imagine why."

Carol smiled politely at the principal's comment, although his voice gave no indication if he intended to make an ironic comment or a perfectly serious observation. "It was kind of you to wait," she said, thinking that it had been an opportunity for him to find out exactly what information she was receiving.

CHAPTER EIGHT

Carol parked on the concrete apron at the front of the station, congratulating herself that she would only be a few minutes late. There was a patrol car next to the dusty sedan, so she assumed that Sergeant Griffin had arrived and was waiting for her.

She drew up beside the lone gum tree. She had just taken the key out of the ignition when the front of the wooden building swelled and burst with a bass roar.

The car rocked, and Carol threw up her arms to protect her face. Debris carried by the shock wave of the explosion rained on the car, cracking the glass in front of her, but not shattering it.

She was out of the car and running. Dust and smoke billowed toward her, carrying the acrid smell of charring wood. She could hear a male voice screaming incoherently.

The door hung on one hinge. Carol pushed past it and almost stumbled over the bulky form lying on its back in front of what was left of the wooden counter. There had been no chance of survival: The face and hands were gone; the trunk a lacerated bleeding mass. Ken Kirk stood over the body, his face contorted, a continuous inhuman wailing coming from his mouth.

Flames flickered in the kindling that had once been the counter. Carol shook the constable's shoulder. "Fire extinguisher — where is it?" He ignored her.

She ran down the corridor that led to the back of the station. Halfway down, the red cylinder of an extinguisher hung on the wall. She heaved it from its mountings and turned it upside down to operational position as she ran back to the front. The gush of foam killed the leaping orange flames almost instantly. Smoke and vapor swirled in circular patterns.

Carol let the heavy metal cylinder thud to the floor. Ken Kirk was still howling, his eyes fixed on the mangled remains at his feet. She quickly checked the constable over — there was no blood on him. "Stop that!" she shouted. When he didn't respond she slapped him hard across the face.

He jerked back and the sound stopped. He stood panting, staring at her. "The Sarge..."

"This is Sergeant Griffin?"

His eyes flickered to the body. His Adam's apple bobbed as he swallowed. "Yes."

"Was there anyone here? What did you see?"

He looked at her uncomprehending. "See?"

"This was a bomb, Constable. Was there a parcel? Did someone deliver something?"

He didn't seem to hear her questions. "The Sarge," he said. "The Sarge said he knew."

"Knew what?"

He shook his head as if to clear it. "The Sarge . . ."

Carol knew he was in shock, but she said harshly, "Tell me!"

But he had fallen silent. She led him, unresisting, outside, her knees suddenly weak with the thought that if she'd been a few minutes earlier she too would be a mass of bleeding flesh on the station floor.

CHAPTER NINE

Carol was late rising, having been up until well after midnight. After police reinforcements from the nearest large town, Harmerville, had arrived to secure the scene, she had had a wrenching hour with Sergeant Griffin's family. His teenage daughter had sobbed continually, but his wife, a plump little woman, tried valiantly to keep her composure and answer Carol's questions.

When Carol had asked if Griffin had ever received any threats, his wife revealed that the day before the sergeant had received an anonymous letter. "Arnie threw it away. He never took it seriously at all."

She remembered that the letter had been typed on a plain sheet of white paper. "It said something about a court and how Arnie had been found guilty of something and how a sentence would be carried out." Her mouth trembled. "I told him he should tell someone, but he just tossed it in the bin . . ."

Carol asked if there had been anything unusual about the letter or the envelope in which it had been posted. "No . . . except when Arnie opened it, a circle cut from yellow paper fell out."

She had shaken her head when Carol asked if there was any chance the letter was still in the rubbish. "The garbage collection's on Wednesday. The bins were all emptied this morning."

Carol had then spoken at length with the Commissioner and Chief Superintendent Healy, the regional commander. Following instructions, she had used the public phone in an alcove off the hotel foyer to contact Trevorwill at ASIO headquarters.

After a few hours of restless sleep filled with fragmented nightmares, morning came too quickly. Following a long hot shower to unkink her back — the sagging mattress had been as uncomfortable as she had feared — she dressed in slacks and a casual jacket. She felt a chill as she slid the guns into their holsters. No firearm could protect her from the force of a blast like the one that had killed Sergeant Griffin.

A forensic team had been flown in from Sydney during the evening, and Carol had left Bourke, who had arrived in town shortly after the explosion, in charge of the crime scene. Ken Kirk had been admitted to the local hospital and was under sedation, but she'd charmed the doctor, a small fussy man, into allowing her a few minutes with the constable, and had been able to extract the fact that Sergeant Griffin had carried in a brown paper parcel from his car when he returned to the station.

Kirk had seen him put it on the front counter, but then the constable had gone to the bathroom and had been there when the bomb exploded. When Carol pressed him for details, Kirk became extremely agitated. His raised voice had brought the doctor, who shooed Carol away.

Now, in the brightness of morning, the dark scene of the sergeant's death was etched in her mind. The pungent smell of scorched flesh seemed to be still in her hair, although she had just shampooed it. She could see the shreds of meat blasted from the body, the blood seeping into the floorboards, the obscenely faceless trunk, shattered arms outstretched.

After making a reassuring call to Aunt Sarah in Sydney, Carol lined up a couple of interviews, and then went downstairs to the dining room. It seemed somehow wrong to feel hungry, but she was ravenous. There were a few people lingering over breakfast, and they looked up as she came through the double glass doors. Denise Cleever was sitting demurely reading a newspaper at a corner table, and Carol's glance slid over her incuriously. They would stage-manage a meeting later.

The hotel dining room was paneled in dark wood to eye height, then the remaining wall area and ceiling were stark white. Four wooden ceiling fans hung motionless. The fifth turned lethargically. The solid chairs had cane backs, and each sturdy table was spread with a white lace tablecloth that reached almost to the floor.

The publican's wife, Beryl Bennett, came hurrying over. Only a few strands of wispy hair were escaping from the tortoiseshell combs, but her soft face already had a harried expression. "Inspector!" she exclaimed, gesturing for Carol to sit at the nearest free table. "Herb tells me you were actually there when it happened!"

By now the others in the room were frankly staring. Carol could imagine the efficacy of the bush telegraph that overnight had conveyed the gruesome details of the death of the town's senior police officer.

"I was just parking my car when the bomb exploded," she said. Normally she wouldn't have confirmed that it *was* a bomb. Convenient explanations of accumulated gas igniting were often used as a cover while evidence was being gathered, but in this case Carol wanted to stir up as much comment and conversation as possible in an effort to uncover every possible lead.

Beryl Bennett handed her a menu, then clasped her hands in front of her generous bust. "No one can believe it. I mean, Arnie Griffin was a lovely man. He did so much good work with kids and the local football team. And he was the life and soul of the historical society. This must be some dreadful mistake. No one would want to hurt him."

She paused to indicate the menu in Carol's hand. "If you want a full breakfast, dear, you'll have to order it right away. Cook'll be off soon."

Passing on her usual light breakfast because she hadn't eaten since the admittedly gargantuan lunch the day before, Carol ordered the hotel's Hearty

Deluxe and black coffee, then sat back to survey the room. A man two tables away was chewing his way through a plate heaped with food. He looked prosperous, supremely self-confident. He was in shirtsleeves, with a flamboyant tie. His dark hair was sleeked back, and his face was newly shaved and pinkly healthy.

He raised a fork to catch her attention. "I say, Inspector Ashton, mind if I join you for a moment?"

At Carol's nodded assent, he leaped to his feet, seized his plate, knife, and fork and strode over to her table. He set these down, said, "Won't be a mo," and went back for his toast, tea, and napkin.

Before he seated himself he shook her hand heartily. "Bob Donnovan here. Progress Association."

She identified him immediately from ASIO background information as the owner of Katamulla's hardware and building supplies store. Of greater interest was the fact that Rick Turner was one of his employees.

Rescuing her fingers from his robust handshake, she said, "I believe your Association's responsible for the success of Bushranger Week. It's received a lot of publicity in Sydney."

"Indeed, yes," he said, organizing his breakfast in front of him. "Most gratifying. Mind if I eat? I mean, you haven't got yours yet."

"Of course not." She watched Donnovan take a large mouthful of eggs and sausage. He paused to shove in a piece of toast, then chewed noisily.

"You had something to tell me, Mr. Donnovan?"

"Bob! You must call me Bob." He took a loud swallow of tea. "Fact is," he said, "I might have been the last one to see Arnie before it happened." He shook his head. "Shocking business. I'd say it's because he was cracking down on drugs, wouldn't you?"

"You said you saw the sergeant . . ."

"I did. Waved to him as we passed on the road. He was coming out of the Cosil-Ross place about half past four. I reckon he'd been visiting. Heard from them yet?"

"Not yet."

Donnovan munched thoughtfully on another forkful. "Good bloke," he said. "Arnie, I mean." He looked regretfully at his empty plate, then scraped a piece of toast around it to mop up any remaining morsels. Gulping down this sustenance, he leaned toward her to breathe, "Drug angle's the way to go. Arnie was keeping the town clean and someone — probably from Sydney — didn't like it."

"Bob giving you his theories?" said a new voice.

Donnovan scraped back his chair and stood. "Well, Lizbeth, I would have thought you'd have collared the Inspector a lot sooner than this."

Carol knew who the woman smiling down at her was from the ASIO briefing file. Lizbeth Hamilton was owner and editor of the district newspaper, the *Katamulla Recorder,* a business she had inherited from her husband. She ran it with the help of her teenage daughter, Becca, who was a close friend of Kent Agar's son, Scott.

As Bob Donnovan introduced them, Carol looked her over. Although dressed in an old pair of jeans and a faded black sloppy joe, Lizbeth Hamilton was undeniably attractive. Her abundant red-brown hair was carelessly pulled back in a ponytail and secured by a thick rubber band. This unceremonious style accentuated the classic bone structure of her face. She had deep blue eyes and dimples that disappeared as her smile faded.

"These are horrible things, Inspector. First poor Dean and Wayne, then Arnie Griffin."

Before Carol could reply, her breakfast was set in front of her. "Let the Inspector eat!" commanded Beryl Bennett. She stacked Donnovan's dishes. "You want something, Lizbeth?"

"I know this is an intrusion," said Lizbeth to Carol, "but if it's okay I'll join you for coffee." She unslung her voluminous shoulder bag and pulled out a chair.

"I'll get along, then," said Donnovan, "and leave you ladies to it." He tapped Carol's shoulder lightly. "Anything I can do . . . Just ask."

Lizbeth Hamilton's face was blank as she watched him walk away, but Carol had a feeling that she disliked Bob Donnovan intensely.

Carol began to eat her breakfast, savoring the tastes of fresh eggs, thick bacon, sausages, and crisply fried potatoes. Neither spoke until the coffee arrived.

Fortified by food and caffeine, Carol asked a few conversational questions about the town and the newspaper. Lizbeth Hamilton gave a self-deprecatory laugh. "Frankly, I'm out of my league with murder. Generally the most dramatic items I cover are traffic accidents or vandalism, with the odd domestic dispute or pub fight."

"You knew Dean Bayliss?"

"Since he was a kid. His family is shattered, of course."

"We're looking for any motive that might be the cause of such brutal murders," said Carol with calculated frankness. "Did you ever hear of Dean being involved with anyone or anything questionable?"

"I wish I could help you, Inspector, but he was just an ordinary young man — not particularly bright, but good-natured."

As Lizbeth had referred to Wayne Bucci by his first name, Carol asked if she had known him well.

"Wayne?" She gazed into her coffee cup. "He was a nice guy. He'd only been in town a few months, but we got to be good mates — he'd often drop into the office and have a chat." She looked up. "Do you have any idea *why*? I can't believe Wayne was mixed up in anything shady."

"Who did he socialize with? Anyone in particular?" Carol willed her to give Rick Turner's name so that she would have a valid reason to question him.

"He got on with everyone — even though he could be a bit extreme." When Carol gave her an interrogative look, Lizbeth went on, "Wayne had these ideas about government conspiracies. I think he seriously believed that individual freedoms were under threat." Her smile had a hint of sadness. "We had a lot of arguments on the topic."

"When did you see him last?"

She didn't hesitate. "Friday afternoon about three. He was with Rick Turner, who called in to give me an ad to run in the paper the next day."

Bingo! thought Carol. Aloud she said, "Rick Turner?"

"Rick has a small farm about twenty minutes out of town." Lizbeth fiddled with a spoon. "I suppose you'll think I'm playing detective, but when I heard about the murders, I asked Rick about Wayne and what happened that afternoon. He said Wayne had some appointment, but didn't give any details. The last Rick saw him was about three-thirty when he dropped him off at Ivy Smith's place, where Wayne rented a room."

Although she already knew the answer from the background file, Carol asked, "Where can I find Mr. Turner?"

"Rick works part-time in the hardware store. You might catch him there." Lizbeth hunted around in her large bag and came up with a dog-eared notebook. "I'm supposed to be interviewing *you,* Inspector," she said, flipping to a blank page. "Since I'm here on the spot, I've already had calls from Sydney asking for my angle on the story."

Her newspaper was distributed throughout the whole district, so Carol wanted to use it to make an appeal for information. Usually she stonewalled the media this early in a case, but this one needed different techniques. "I'm happy to give an interview," she said, "but I think I'll have more information later today. Perhaps I could drop over to your office this afternoon?"

Lizbeth Hamilton closed her notebook. "That's a promise, I hope? I've got a deadline of four o'clock for tomorrow's edition." She smiled. "But I'll hold the front page for *you,* Inspector."

"I'll call you if there's any problem."

"Perhaps Becca can take a photo of you?" She added with obvious pride, "My daughter. I'm teaching her the ropes."

"I'd rather you concentrated on photos of the victims. It may jog someone's memory."

Sobered by Carol's request, Lizbeth said, "Are you buying Donnovan's idea that drugs are behind the murders?"

"I'm not buying anything, yet. What do you think?"

Lizbeth leaned her elbows on the table and rested her chin on her clenched hands. "There's something going on here in Katamulla," she said quietly. "I hear rumors, stories . . . But nothing definite." She gave a rueful smile. "Perhaps you'll think I'm out of my tree, but there's something going on here and it's . . ." Embarrassed, she faltered, then finished, ". . . it's evil. I'm sure that sounds awfully melodramatic, but that's the way it is."

They both looked up as Mark Bourke came up to the table. He looked exhausted and hadn't shaved. Carol introduced him to Lizbeth Hamilton, and he gave a friendly smile as he made an easy comment. Carol always admired Bourke's informal, relaxed style. He seemed so ordinary, so unthreatening, but many had found to their cost that his casual manner hid a keen mind and a steely tenacity.

Lizbeth excused herself, and Bourke sank gratefully into her seat. "I'm bloody tired," he said. "I need a shave, a shower, and a couple of hours sleep." He yawned as he checked the now almost deserted dining room. Satisfied that they couldn't be overheard, he went on, "The team's on the way back to Sydney with what looks like a thousand plastic bags of evidence, including countless paper fragments. They'll try to reconstruct some of the documents, but if there was anything on interviews he'd done for us, I think we can kiss them good-bye."

"Was the bomb definitely in the parcel that Griffin brought into the station?"

"Looks that way. We'll get a formal report, but it's pretty well confirmed that plastic explosive was used. It only needed a simple pressure trigger, so that the first person who opened it would be blown sky-high."

Smothering another yawn, he went on, "And four guys have arrived from regional headquarters. Two of them, Rush and Millet, have been assigned to our investigation, and the other two are here to officially take over the station. None too soon — the networks are onto it. When I left they were just starting to arrive, including 'The Shipley Report's' forward troops."

He smiled broadly as Beryl Bennett appeared with a steaming teapot covered by a purple knitted cozy and a plate of toast. "Thanks, Beryl. You've saved my life!"

"No trouble, dear." She beamed at him and hurried away.

"Beryl, is it?" said Carol, amused. "Already?"

"Never hurts to be friendly," said Bourke. "The pub's the social center of the town." He took a huge bite of buttered toast and gave a blissful groan. "I really need this."

"I've spoken to the Commissioner," Carol said quietly. "Both he and the ASIO brass agree that the murders and the bombing are connected, particularly in light of the yellow disk that was in the letter Griffin received."

"I've checked, and we've got absolutely no chance of locating that letter. Garbage collected goes straight to the council dump, where they've got machinery running all day covering everything with dirt."

"We still have to take into account the possibility that the sergeant's death might be related to some other local investigation," said Carol. "Use the officers assigned to us to check through the files that survived the explosion and to trace the steps in Griffin's day. I want to know everywhere he went and everyone he saw before he came back to the station at five. Tell them to particularly ask if anyone noticed him with a brown paper parcel at any stage."

"We're staying with the drug story as a cover?"

"Absolutely. I'll follow that line when I do the interview with the local paper this afternoon." She smiled at his tired face. "And I've some good news for you — I've assigned Anne Newsome to the case to take some of the load off you. When she arrives later this morning, tell her to follow up the list of teacher contacts I got yesterday, except for Gwen Pickard — I'll do her. Anne can yank them out of class, if necessary. If the principal complains, I'll deal with him."

"On the subject of contacts," said Bourke as he picked up the purple-clad teapot, "I did see a rather attractive woman on the way in. I may well chat her up later."

Carol had to smile at the thought of Bourke making overtures to Denise Cleever. "Don't ham it up too much, Mark. It needs to look natural."

"I'll act so natural even you'll be convinced." He looked approvingly at the steaming amber tea as it poured into his cup. "Speaking of acting, are you convinced that Constable Kirk is dinkum? The lucky bastard certainly chose the right time to take a leak."

"It's possible he knows something. At the scene he was in complete shock, and it didn't seem to be an act. He did say one cryptic thing — 'The Sarge said he knew . . .' and then he clammed up. Later at the hospital he went to pieces when I questioned him. It seems to be more than just the trauma of the explosion. After you've had a rest, I'd like you to see what you can get out of him. If man-to-man doesn't work, lean on him, hard."

"Inspector," said Beryl Bennett from the doorway. "Phone call for you. Would you like to take it at the front desk?"

"Before I forget to tell you," Bourke said as Carol pushed back her chair, "that leak from the morgue . . . you were right, it *was* that doctor, Jeanine Price."

"Her own idea to get a little cash on the side?"

"She didn't think of it first. Price says she was approached by phone and well paid to contact the media outlets. She claims she doesn't know who, or why, or anything else. The money was delivered on schedule in an unmarked envelope left at her home. You know, Carol, someone's going to a lot of trouble to get maximum publicity."

Leaving him to finish his toast and tea, Carol went out into the dimly lit foyer and picked up the receiver lying on the green blotter in the center of the counter. Beryl Bennett was concentrating on the guest register, although Carol was sure she was listening.

The voice on the line was low, cultured, faintly

amused. "Inspector Ashton? This is Elaine Cosil-Ross. I do wonder if you could spare the time to join my brother and me for lunch here, at our home. I believe we may have been almost the last people to see poor Sergeant Griffin alive."

When Carol put down the receiver, Beryl, obviously impressed, said, "Did you know the Cosil-Rosses are the most important family in the district? The family's been here since the town began."

"I saw the name on the front of the school hall."

"Oh, *yes*," said Beryl approvingly, "they've been very generous."

Carol lingered to say casually, "I believe the Agars are another well-established family."

Leaning comfortably on the counter, Beryl settled herself for a chat. "Kent's our member of parliament, and he's done his best for us there. What's more, he's never forgotten his roots, if you know what I mean. Not like some of them." She dropped her voice confidingly. "His wife doesn't fit in. Never did. Nothing's ever been good enough for Maggie Agar. Made him tear down the old homestead and put up a great big white house with tennis courts and a swimming pool." She clicked her tongue in disapproval. "Eyesore, that's what it is."

After a pause for Carol to absorb this, she added in a doleful tone, "Is it any wonder there's trouble in the marriage?"

"Trouble?" Carol prompted.

"Kent's taken to spending as much time as possible in Sydney, whether or not parliament's sitting. If you ask me, Maggie's just driven him too far. You wouldn't think to look at her, but she's someone you should never cross." She raised her eyebrows knowingly. "The still-waters-run-deep sort, dear."

Herb Bennett put his head around the door to the bar. "Beryl..." he reproached.

"Oops, dear. Got to go."

Carol found Bourke squeezing a last half-cup from the teapot. "Mark, after you see Kirk at the hospital, go to the bakery where Dean Bayliss worked. I've spoken to the owner by phone, but you might come up with something more. And since Lizbeth Hamilton's confirmed that Rick Turner was with Bucci on Friday afternoon, you might try to locate him so we can see him together later today. He works at the hardware store."

"Good-bye, sleep," said Bourke with resignation. His fingers made a rasping sound as he rubbed his unshaven cheek. "You're seeing Agar's kid this morning?"

Carol looked at her watch. "Yes, in about half an hour. Then I'll check out Ivy Smith, who rented Wayne Bucci a room. And I've just been invited to lunch by Elaine Cosil-Ross, which should be interesting, because it seems that she and her brother were the last people, apart from Kirk, to see Griffin alive."

Bourke raised his eyebrows. "Local landed gentry," he said. "Be sure to tug your forelock in a suitably servile fashion."

CHAPTER TEN

The rental car Carol was driving while the cracked windscreen in her vehicle was replaced was a white Ford with an irritating scent of fake-leather spray that apparently had been employed in an attempt to disguise the smell of cigarette smoke. Even though it was chilly and overcast, she wound down the window to a blast of cool air as she took the road that crossed the Boolworrie River and ran south out of town.

After three kilometers the Agar house flashed ostentatiously into view. The bulky three-story edifice lived up to Beryl Bennett's disparaging description. The architect had apparently been instructed to recreate a European minicastle in the Australian countryside, ignoring how incongruous it would look on its perch overlooking the robust beauty of the Katamulla Valley. Its battlements and towers were painted a blinding white. Three flagpoles carried respectively a jumbo Australian flag, the Union Jack, and an elaborate heraldic design. Carol had the sardonic thought that this was undoubtedly Kent Agar's flashy version of a family coat of arms.

Kent Agar's wife, Maggie, didn't fit the picture Carol had formed. She was slim, soft voiced, and wore a pale blue skirt and white sweater. These toned with the neutral shade of her brown shoulder-length hair and lightly tanned, rather wistful face. She offered Carol a limp hand and then led her down a wide hallway to a sitting room adjoining a large kitchen where an array of pots and pans hung suspended from the ceiling on huge black hooks.

"Scott, this is Inspector Ashton. She's come to see you."

Barefoot and wearing tattered jeans and a T-shirt, her son was sprawled on a striped couch surrounded by textbooks and papers. On top of a pile of books a metal ashtray with a half-smoked cigarette vied for space with an open can of beer.

Scott Agar got to his feet reluctantly, brushing ash from his jeans. He was a taller, blander version of his father, with the same small features and high-arched eyebrows, but his auburn hair was thick and his mouth was wider and weaker. "Hi. Find somewhere to sit." His tone was surly.

Maggie Agar cleared a low upholstered chair for

Carol, then collected a tall stool from the kitchen and placed it nearby. Sitting upright on the stool, she loomed over Carol. "You won't mind if I stay, Inspector?"

"Of course not. These are just routine questions." To Scott, she said pleasantly, "You're not at school today."

"Studying." He sat down, took a long drag at his cigarette, and left it dangling from his lower lip. "Got exams soon."

"Take that cigarette out of your mouth," said his mother quietly. He shot her a look, then stubbed it out in the ashtray.

Folding his arms, he declared, "I told Sergeant Griffin on the phone I didn't know anything."

"You didn't see him in person?"

Maggie Agar said smoothly, "Scott was studying. I didn't see any point in having Griffin come here."

Carol said to Scott, "You've heard about the explosion at the police station?"

"Yeah." He leaned over to take a swallow from his can of beer.

"We were shocked, of course," Maggie Agar interposed. "It seems incredible that violence like this can occur in Katamulla." She shook her head slowly to indicate how regrettable it all was.

This is an act, Carol thought.

Taking out her notebook, she asked for the names of Dean's friends and acquaintances. Scott sighed elaborately, but with an occasional prompt from his mother, he complied. After a series of questions about the interests and activities Dean and Scott shared, Carol said, "His body was found with that of another man who had been living in town." She passed each of them a photograph of a smiling Wayne Bucci. "Do you recognize him?"

"I'm sorry." Maggie Agar handed the photo back to Carol. "I don't recall the man."

Scott studied his copy closely. "I dunno," he said at last, "I might have seen him around . . ."

"His name was Wayne Bucci."

"This is a small town, Inspector," said Maggie Agar with a facile smile. "It's quite likely that Scott would recognize this man merely from passing him in the street."

"He was seen in the company of a man called Rick Turner on Friday afternoon. Do either of you know Mr. Turner?"

Scott Agar nodded. "Yeah, I know him — but not well." His mother ignored the question.

Carol displayed an illustration of a brown Volvo station wagon. "How about this particular model and color?"

"There are plenty of Volvos in the district," Maggie Agar said quickly. "I imagine both Scott and I know several that could fit that description."

Carol looked at Scott. He glanced at his mother, then shrugged. "Doesn't ring a bell."

Watching him closely, Carol passed him a shot showing both sides of the Saint Christopher medallion found under Dean's body. "Does this seem familiar?"

His eyes widened involuntarily. He handed it back to her quickly. "Never seen it before."

"Would you take another look, please. Perhaps you've seen someone wearing it."

Maggie Agar was on her feet. "Perhaps I can help." She examined the photograph, then returned it to Carol. "I'm sorry."

Scott was watching his mother. "Mum . . . ?"

Her expression stony, she said, "Go back to your work."

She turned to Carol. "I think, Inspector, that will be enough. Scott has a lot of studying to do. If you have any further questions, my husband will be here during the weekend."

Carol allowed herself to be ushered out of the house. Scott Agar had been shaken by the picture of the medallion, and she wanted him to stew a little before she interviewed him again.

As she drove back into town she reviewed the list of names Scott Agar had given her. Two stood out. The first was Eliot Donnovan, the son of the man who had invited himself to breakfast with her that morning. The second was Becca Hamilton, the newspaper proprietor's daughter. Scott had said she was Dean Bayliss's steady girlfriend, and Carol wondered why Lizbeth Hamilton hadn't mentioned that to her.

Carol had an unsatisfactory interview with Ivy Smith, a small vague woman who seemed completely bewildered by the comings and goings of her tenant. "I *think* I saw Wayne on Friday night, you know, but I *could* be wrong . . . Wait! I *did* run into him in the evening . . . No, that would have been Thursday . . . And I didn't really notice Wayne wasn't there on the weekend, because, you see, I spent the time with my sister over in Harmerville . . . Of course, I did come back *early*, but Wayne spent a lot of time out, and I wouldn't have *expected* to see him... and I don't think I did..."

Doubting that even Bourke's patience could contend with this level of earnest uncertainty, Carol abandoned her questions, thanked the waffling little woman, and went back to her car no wiser.

Following the detailed instructions from Elaine Cosil-Ross, Carol drove deep into the countryside. A high wind was tearing open the cloud cover, and the dull day was enlivened by patches of dazzling sunlight dancing over the low hills. After about thirty minutes of driving on back roads through heavy bushland alternating with green paddocks dotted with cattle, Carol caught sight of black wrought-iron gates that proclaimed in ornate metal letters, THE GRANGE. The barbed wire fencing that stretched on either side had warning signs at intervals indicating that it was electrified.

Inside the gate a Land Rover was waiting, a woman sitting behind the wheel, a man leaning relaxed against the door, smoking a pipe. This must be Stuart Cosil-Ross, who was married to Rick Turner's sister. He seemed to Carol rather formally dressed for the setting, with obviously expensive tan slacks and fine wool sweater. Carol's arrival galvanized him into action. He knocked out his pipe, pointed a remote control to open the gate, and then hurried over to Carol's car.

"My sister and I are delighted to see you, Inspector," he said expansively, gesturing toward the woman who was now standing beside the four-wheel drive. "Just go through and park over to the side there. We'll take you down in the Land Rover. The road down's a bit difficult, particularly after the rain we had yesterday."

Carol parked in the indicated place, grabbed her shoulder bag, and slid out of the car. The black metal gate closed with an emphatic click as she locked the driver's door. Elaine Cosil-Ross said with a small smile, "That's not really necessary, Inspector. Your car will be quite safe." She was wearing an outfit comparable to her brother's — a skirt and sweater that suggested well-bred, understated expense.

Only a few streaks of fresh wet mud marred the shining surfaces of the Land Rover, which was obviously new. Elaine Cosil-Ross put Carol into the front passenger seat and slid in behind the wheel. Stuart Cosil-Ross clambered into the back. Leaning between the seats, he explained, "Put you there so you can have a good view. It's quite a sight, when we start going down."

It was obvious that Elaine and Stuart Cosil-Ross were closely related. They shared the same lanky build, fine brown hair, arrogant nose, and large, dark eyes, but Stuart had a soft set to his mouth and a friendly manner. His sister was more reserved, but Carol didn't think it was shyness that restrained her, but cool aloofness.

It took more than fifteen minutes to get to the homestead. The road, graded dirt with loose gravel laid over it, ran level for a short time, then plunged down a steep incline. "You can see why we met you at the top," said Stuart.

Carol could. The road was cut deep into the hillside, zigzagging its way through virgin bushland down to the floor of the valley below. There was no guardrail, and the drop was precipitous. At several points dirt and rocks had washed across the surface, and Elaine was forced to slow to a walking pace to negotiate each hazard. Carol wouldn't like to have driven it at night, and said so.

"Piece of cake!" said Stuart. "Once you know it, and you've got a four-wheel drive, it's nothing to worry about, even if it's pitch black. All you've got to do is watch out you don't hit a kangaroo or wombat — they come out at night."

Remembering what Denise had told her about the death of the environmentalist Neal Rudin, who had accused the Cosil-Ross family of failing to conserve protected species, Carol said, "I've heard you've got a koala colony on your land."

"Colony?" said Elaine Cosil-Ross disdainfully, as the Land Rover jolted over gravel and small boulders. "There's a few koalas scattered around. I wouldn't dignify the numbers with the word *colony*."

They came around a final hairpin bend. "Look there!" exclaimed Stuart. He began a proud description of the homestead as they dropped toward the broad floor of the valley. Heavily timbered slopes surrounded the well-tended paddocks where cattle grazed. A flock of black cockatoos, disturbed by their passing, wheeled and shrieked above them.

As they drove down an avenue of poplars, almost leafless at this time of year, the sun came out like a well-timed spotlight, illuminating the graceful building and its landscaped surroundings. Though constructed on a grand scale, it was a traditional country homestead, built for function, not esthetics. Set on a rise above the curving line of weeping willows that marked a watercourse, it melded with its environment in a way that the Agar monstrosity never could. The building was constructed of local timber, with a deep red corrugated iron roof, and wide veranda on each side. An enclosed garden skirted the front where stone steps led to the main entrance, but Carol was sure that the country custom of using the back door would apply.

A weathered wooden barn with a red roof that matched the main house stood to one side. Behind it an orchard stretched down to the river flats. As if on cue, a flock of white geese appeared, marching self-importantly in formation as the Land Rover crunched to a stop on the crushed river gravel that formed the driveway.

"Watchgeese," said Stuart with obvious pleasure. "My idea — instead of dogs. I'd advise you to stay close by me. If they sense a stranger, they'll run at you, hissing. Can give a nasty bite."

He opened the door and put up a hand to help Carol out. Up close, the geese were bulky birds with large webbed feet, beady stares, and formidable flat beaks. The leader examined Carol closely, then spread his considerable wings, pushed his head forward, and hissed loudly.

Elaine Cosil-Ross clapped her hands, and the goose subsided. He stalked off, his flock following him. Elaine frowned at her brother. "Honestly, Stuart," she said severely, "I think you enjoy frightening visitors." She smiled at Carol. "Not that Inspector Ashton seems the slightest intimidated."

They entered the house, as Carol had expected, through the back of the building where a large vegetable garden was bursting with greenery. On the veranda gum boots of various sizes were lined up beside the kitchen door, and a collection of coats hung from wooden pegs above them. There was an indefinable, pleasant odor that Carol always associated with the country — a combination of the scents of animals and hay and ripening fruit and the earthy smell of rich soil.

Elaine opened the door, which was unlocked. The kitchen was large and airy. The appliances were modern, but the huge wooden kitchen table was so old that its surface was worn into dips and hollows, and the cabinets lining the walls were originals, with old-fashioned spring catches and wire mesh inserts to allow air to circulate to the shelves.

"Stuart, if you'll get our guest a drink, I'll organize lunch."

It was obvious Stuart's wife wasn't there. Wondering where Hannah Cosil-Ross was, Carol followed him through to a parlor that was, she realized, a shrine to the Cosil-Ross family. Glass cases held mementos and heirlooms, from beautiful lace christening robes to flintlock pistols. The walls were crowded with photographs and paintings. The distinctive Cosil-Ross face stared out from every frame in a history that stretched from the faded sepia images of the nineteenth century through to the modern portraits in oil of Elaine and Stuart themselves.

Stuart didn't ask Carol what she wanted to drink, but handed her a dry sherry in a crystal glass. Picking up his own drink, he looked around with satisfaction. "Quite a family, eh?"

Her attention was taken by a faded map of the property hanging in a heavy frame over the mantelpiece. Seeing her interest, Stuart said, "The original grant, and we've still got pretty much the

121

same boundaries. Not like most holdings, where over the years the land's been cut up and sold. Our family made a lot of money early, and kept it."

Carol examined the map closely. The property was a huge oval, running west-east, and taking in an entire valley. A permanent water supply was indicated by the blue line of the river snaking through the center. Beside the river, deep in the valley, was a heavily hatched area. "What's this?" she asked, pointing.

Stuart peered at the map, then stepped back with a satisfied smile. "I mentioned money — that's where it came from. The workmen's huts and the furnaces are in ruins, of course, but that's where kerosene shale, mined nearby, was crushed and heated to extract the fuel. Went out of business when electricity came through, but by that time the Cosil-Ross family had their financial foundation."

Carol studied the map, mentally comparing it to the contour map she had of the whole Katamulla district. "This river that flows through the property, it's a tributary of the Boolworrie isn't it? So that means your northern border is the Boolworrie National Park."

"Very good, Inspector! I can see you've been doing your homework."

"The way I came in today isn't shown on this map."

"No, that was put in much later when this homestead was built in the twenties." He indicated a faded red square at the western end of the property. "Here's the first farmhouse and the original road. It's an easier gradient, so we use it to get stock and produce in and out, but it's too far away to use as a main entrance."

The area he indicated seemed ideal for militia maneuvers, so Carol said casually, "Do you use the farmhouse at all?"

"Of course. The farmhands and seasonal workers sleep there. It's really very comfortable, considering it was built last century."

Apparently convinced that Carol would be as fascinated with the Cosil-Ross family as he was himself, Stuart began a long rambling dissertation on his forebears that Carol short-circuited with a blunt statement.

"Mr. Cosil-Ross, I'm here because of three violent deaths. Your sister said on the phone she believed you two may have been the last to see Sergeant Griffin before he returned to the station and was killed."

Stuart carefully put his crystal glass down on a coaster. "Dreadful business," he said. "Parcel bomb, I believe."

"Why was Sergeant Griffin here?"

Stuart shrugged. "You'll have to ask Elaine. It was nothing to do with me. I only saw him at the top gate as he was leaving." He gulped down the last of his sherry and moved to the door. "Excuse me, Elaine will want me to set the table . . ."

Carol followed him into the dining room, which was full of heavy dark furniture. Before she could ask another question, Elaine Cosil-Ross said from the doorway, "Do be seated, Inspector. I hope you don't mind simple, home-cooked food."

The first course was split pea and ham soup

served with slabs of crusty homemade bread. As Stuart cleared the plates, Carol said, "You're involved in local politics?"

Elaine looked surprised at the question. "Of course. I've always believed that it's important to give something to the community."

"I believe you're on Kent Agar's reelection committee."

"She runs it," said Stuart proudly. "If you ask me, Elaine's the reason he maintains such a big majority." He smiled indulgently at his sister. "She's even got him involved in the Bushranger Week festivities this weekend."

"I'm afraid Kent's canceled," said Elaine, her voice frosty. "For some reason he's unable to attend."

"But he's the key speaker . . ."

"We'll just have to get along without him." It was obvious from her tone that the subject was closed.

The main course was steak and kidney pie and creamy mashed potatoes. Looking at the size of the helping on her plate, Carol made a mental promise to eat a light dinner and go for a run in the morning.

"Now, Inspector," said Elaine Cosil-Ross crisply, "you've been very patient, but I'm sure you're anxious to know about Sergeant Griffin's visit here yesterday." She took a sip of her wine. "The fact is, I asked him to call in because I had some evidence for him."

"Of a crime?"

"You might call it that. Unfortunately we've been plagued in this area with vandals — youths who get their entertainment by driving out into the country to take potshots at anything that takes their fancy." Her mouth tightened. "I believe in responsible gun ownership, but these young hoodlums are going to kill someone before they've finished. They seem to think it's fun to blaze away at road signs, transformers, even stock in the paddocks."

Carol said, "And you could identify these youths?"

"I've kept a log of the incidents, descriptions of the vehicles and, in two cases, photographs where they were caught in the act. I turned these over to Sergeant Griffin and asked him to take whatever action was appropriate."

"Could you give me some names?"

Her brother broke in before she could reply. "Didn't you say Bob Donnovan's son was one of them, Elaine?"

She shot him a look of impatient anger. "I didn't say any such thing. I *did* mention Scott Agar. I'm sure he's one of the ringleaders."

"Kent Agar's son?" said Carol with a deliberate tone of surprise. "Surely you would have approached his father directly over this matter?"

"You understand, Inspector, it was rather a delicate matter. I preferred to leave the whole problem with Sergeant Griffin."

"The material you collected, the logs and photographs, when you gave them to the sergeant, were they in an envelope or a package?"

Elaine's laugh bubbled with genuine merriment. "Why, Inspector," she said, "don't tell me you suspect that *I* gave Sergeant Griffin a parcel bomb!"

CHAPTER ELEVEN

When Carol walked in the hotel's entrance, she was waylaid by a flustered Beryl Bennett. "Inspector, you'll never guess! Madeline Shipley's staying here!" She indicated the register. "She checked in half an hour ago."

Carol said casually that Madeline was a friend, and asked her room number.

"I put her in Pink. Top of the stairs and to the left right to the end of the hall. Number twenty-one. It's a bit out of the way, but it's the best we could do on such short notice." She smiled broadly. "What with the bombing and Bushranger Week beginning this weekend, we're quite full!"

"I'm expecting one of my officers —"

Beryl didn't let her finish. "Lovely young lady! She's in thirty. She put her stuff in her room and went off with Sergeant Bourke."

Carol thanked her and went upstairs, finding room twenty-one without difficulty. When there was no answer to her knock she scribbled a note to ask Madeline if they could meet for an early dinner, and pushed it under the door.

Beryl was still at the desk when she came downstairs again, and was delighted to give her directions to Bob Donnovan's hardware store and the *Katamulla Recorder*. "You can walk from here. Just around the corner. You can't miss them — both on the same side of the street."

Carol leaned an elbow on the counter. "I gather Lizbeth Hamilton took over the business when her husband died..."

Beryl took the cue that Carol was in a chatty mood. "It was awful," she confided. "He hanged himself in the garage. Lizbeth found the body." She shook her head. "Depressed over financial problems, I heard."

"There's a daughter, isn't there?"

"Becca. Spitting image of her mother. Lizbeth wants her to get involved in the paper, but I don't know if that'll work out."

Trusting that her expression conveyed an appropriate desire to gossip, Carol said, "This morning when I saw Maggie Agar, she mentioned that Becca and Dean Bayliss were an item."

"They did go out, but..." Beryl dropped her voice

to an off-the-record murmur, "...I know for a fact that Lizbeth was against it from the start. She thought Dean didn't have any ambition, working in a bakery. Didn't think he was near good enough for her daughter. Frankly, Lizbeth had her eye on Scott Agar for Becca."

"I've had conflicting reports about Dean Bayliss. What did you think about him?"

Beryl pursed her lips. "He was a nice kid, but Dean had a wild side, there's no question about it."

Encouraged by Carol's look of inquiry, she continued, "There're troublemakers in every town, you know, and Katamulla's got their share. Dean was okay — he worked hard, I'll give him that — but he was easily influenced."

"Anyone in particular?"

Unwilling for a moment, Beryl finally said, "Well, although Bob Donnovan's a real asset to Katamulla, I can't say the same for his son, Eliot. If there's any trouble, he'll be in it."

"I did hear a name this morning," said Carol, innocent faced. "Rick Turner. Do you know him?"

"I know Rick. He's never amounted to much, although you wouldn't think that to hear him talk. Although he's well into his twenties, he kicks around with kids much younger than he is, including Dean. Makes him feel like a big man, I suppose."

"His sister's married to Stuart Cosil-Ross, isn't she?"

"For the moment." Beryl's doleful expression indicated she was privy to further information.

Carol said, "At lunch — she wasn't at the homestead. I wondered..."

"Frankly, I never thought it would work. I mean,

Elaine didn't approve, and she's always ruled her brother with an iron rod. And Hannah — I've got nothing against her personally, you understand — she just isn't Cosil-Ross material. It was only a matter of time."

"So they've just separated recently?"

"Only last week, I heard."

They chatted for a few more minutes, but it was obvious Beryl didn't know any further details, so Carol extricated herself and went to find Bob Donnovan's store.

Preparations were in hand for Bushranger Week, which was to begin with a parade on Saturday. Colored bunting was being strung across the main street and wooden barricades were set up to restrain the expected spectators. Carol was wryly amused to see a television crew busily filming the activity. It seemed to her that the murders, coupled with a bombing, had done more to garner publicity for the celebrations than any public relations campaign could hope to achieve.

Bob Donnovan's store was obviously prospering. The parking area at the back was full of cars and trucks, and customers prowled the hardware aisles and building material racks. Donnovan himself was serving in the plumbing section. He looked up from the cash register. "Inspector! I'll be with you in a minute."

Carol idly studied the esoteric plumbing implements displayed, aware she was the subject of curiosity. She had no doubt that her movements in Katamulla were general knowledge. Some people looked at her openly, but most gave her sideways glances.

Her presence in Katamulla had coincided with the bombing, and now she was asking questions and probing the enclosed world of the town. And this was only the beginning of Katamulla's trials. When the full glare of media attention was turned on them, stones would be overturned, secrets revealed, privacies violated.

"Now, what can I do for you?" Bob Donnovan seemed fully as hearty and enthusiastic as he had at breakfast, although the collar of his white shirt had wilted a little, and his garish tie was loosened.

"Is there somewhere private we could talk?"

He was immediately concerned. "Is there something wrong?" He looked around. "There's a tearoom back here. Would that do?"

He led the way past a glass-walled office where two women sat at gleaming computers. "The way to go," he said, gesturing. "We're on-line, up with the latest. You've got to be a step ahead of the competition in this business."

The tearoom was a contrast to the sleek computer office. It was a small, cluttered space with a silver urn steaming to itself and dirty mugs and plates piled in a tiny sink.

"Sit here, Inspector." Donnovan snatched up a pile of colored brochures for roofing materials. "Now, what's the problem?"

Carol waited until he had seated himself across from her. "I was wondering," she said, "what you were doing out near the Cosil-Ross place yesterday afternoon, when you saw Sergeant Griffin."

"Doing? I don't understand."

"I was out there today, and I realized that it's nowhere near a main road. In fact, it's really quite

130

out of the way. Apart from the Grange, there doesn't seem to be any reason to be on the road."

Donnovan ran a hand over his dark hair. Apparently embarrassed, he was silent for a moment, then he said, "Boolworrie National Park's out that way."

"You were visiting the park?" Carol made sure her skepticism was obvious. "Late on a Wednesday afternoon?"

He played with his tie, tightening the knot against his collar. "This is a high-pressure business, you know," he said with a bluff laugh. "I need to relax. Every now and then I just take off — I don't tell anyone, I just go. It just so happens I decided to drive that way yesterday."

"Did you stop and talk with the sergeant?"

"No, I just waved to him as I drove past the gate."

"Was he alone?"

Donnovan seemed anxious to end the interview. He slid to the edge of his chair and checked his watch. "Stuart was there, I think," he said briskly. "I really must get back . . ."

"Your son knew Dean Bayliss."

Subdued, he sank back in his chair. "What's Eliot got to do with this?"

"I'd like to speak with him, Mr. Donnovan."

"He doesn't know anything that would help you."

The facile words came easily. "Merely routine questions," said Carol with a placatory smile. "Just covering the bases, as you might say. We're seeing everybody who knew Bayliss. That's the only reason your son's on my list."

Mollified, he nodded slowly. "Of course we'll

cooperate, but he's at school at the moment. Perhaps tomorrow?"

"I'd rather do it immediately, then it's over and done with. If I have your permission, I'd like to see him this afternoon."

Carol's persistence clearly irritated him, but he reluctantly agreed. When she asked him about the medallion and the station wagon, he shook his head, not bothering to hide his impatience. "Never seen them before."

As she followed him back into the store, she said, "Did you know Wayne Bucci?"

"Who? Oh, the other man who was killed . . . No, never met him, as far as I know."

"You might have seen him at the pub."

Donnovan's joviality was returning. He waved to a customer, "Hey, Ron — be with you in a moment." To Carol he said, "Nice to see you, Inspector."

Carol didn't believe this for a moment.

She strolled to the *Recorder*'s office, enjoying the clean air and leisurely traffic, which actually stopped for pedestrians rather than indulging in Sydney's run-them-down attitude.

Lizbeth Hamilton wasn't in, but her daughter was. She looked up as Carol opened one side of the double doors that had brass push plates and KATAMULLA RECORDER incised into the glass panels.

Carol introduced herself. "And you must be Becca. Your mother told me you're a photographer."

The girl nodded warily. She was, as Beryl Bennett had said, the image of her mother. Her shiny red-brown hair was shorter, and she was a little taller and heavier, but she had the same clean bone structure and blue eyes.

132

However, in contrast to Lizbeth's energy, Becca Hamilton was listless and pale, and when she spoke her voice was a monotone. "Mum's not here. She'll be back soon, if you want to wait."

"I wonder if I could look at last Saturday's paper?"

Becca indicated several papers attached to wooden spines that lay on a slanted desk near the door. "It'll be over there."

The *Recorder*'s office wasn't exactly what Carol had expected. She had pictured it full of old-fashioned printing presses and the smell of ink. Instead, although the building itself was carefully preserved, from the swing doors to the long oak counter that ran the full length of the shop, the equipment she could see seemed extremely modern. She wondered if Lizbeth Hamilton's husband had carried a policy with a suicide waiver that had provided enough money for her to modernize.

Carol found the correct issue and carried it over to where Becca sat. Spreading it on the counter, she said, "Rick Turner ran an advertisement last Saturday. I don't suppose you know which one it was?"

"Sure." Becca flipped over several pages and indicated an advertisement at the top of a column. "That's it. Rick puts it in every few weeks."

FUN WAR GAMES was contained in a simple half-circle logo. The text ran, *Exciting. Challenging. Test Yourself in Safe Combat Situations. All Equipment Provided.* The ad went on to give further information covering the rental of equipment, finishing with details of place and time — eight o'clock on Sunday.

"Where is this?" asked Carol, pointing at the assembly point indicated.

"At the back of Rick's place." She shoved the newspaper away. "It's so stupid," she said with the first sign of animation Carol had seen. "They go out in the bush and play dumb games with paintball guns." Her mouth turned down in derision. "Fuckwits," she added bitingly.

"Did Dean Bayliss join in these war games?"

Becca became very still. "I don't know what you mean."

"He was your boyfriend, wasn't he? That's what I've been told. I thought you'd know his friends, what he did in his spare time..."

The girl's face suddenly crumpled. "We were supposed to go out last Saturday," she said through her tears. "He promised when I saw him on Friday, but I never saw him again."

"What time did you see him on Friday?"

Becca fished in the pocket of her jeans and found a tissue. Dabbing at her eyes, she said, "I don't know... about six o'clock. I met him at the Imperial, and he said he was going to spend Saturday helping Rick set up things for the war games on Sunday, but he'd be back in plenty of time."

"What did you do when Dean didn't turn up?"

"I called Rick's place, and his sister said that Dean and the others were having a barbie and I'd better forget going out." Tears filled her eyes again. "He promised..."

"Rick's sister was there?"

"I suppose..." She gave a hiccuping sob and stood up to search the back pockets of her jeans. Retrieving another tissue, she blew her nose.

Carol said, "Do you have any idea who else might have been at this barbecue Dean mentioned?"

A shrug. "The guys he hangs around with." With a flash of spirit, she added, "Like, I wasn't about to ask, since he'd just stood me up."

Carol took out her notebook and ran Becca through the list of names she'd been given by Scott Agar. Becca nodded. "Could have been any of them. They're always hanging together."

"Would Scott have been there?"

"Maybe. Why don't you ask him yourself?" Her tone was just short of insolent.

Lizbeth Hamilton came through the doors in a whirl of energy. "Oh, great! You're here, Inspector." She frowned at her daughter. "Haven't you offered Inspector Ashton afternoon tea?"

When Carol said she didn't want anything, Lizbeth announced she needed a cup of tea and sent her daughter to the back of the shop to make it for her.

"I hadn't realized that Dean Bayliss was your daughter's boyfriend," said Carol.

"*Boyfriend*'s a bit strong — they knew each other." Lizbeth held open a panel in the counter to allow Carol through. "Frankly, I didn't think he was ever going to account for much, so I discouraged Becca from getting involved with him."

Following Lizbeth into her office, which was more an alcove off the main room, Carol said, "And she took your advice?" She kept her tone light. "Kids her age aren't renowned for that."

Lizbeth looked at her quite seriously. "Becca knows I only want the best for her. That's why she does what I tell her to."

As Lizbeth set up a miniature tape recorder on the desk, she asked, "You don't mind if I tape our interview for the paper, do you? We'll get through it much faster."

The phone on her desk rang, and Lizbeth excused herself to answer it. "It's for you, Inspector."

Bourke was succinct. "Rick Turner's disappeared. He didn't turn up for work on Monday. No one's seen him since Saturday. And we've got another no-show. I couldn't locate Constable Kirk anywhere. I've put an all points out on Turner and I've got someone out checking Kirk's friends."

CHAPTER TWELVE

Carol picked up her car from the hotel and drove straight to the high school. A chatty woman from the office, who introduced herself as Wendy, took her to the principal's office. The door was closed. Indicating a chair, she said to Carol, "He's got a kid with him at the moment, Inspector — little twerp shoved a classmate's head in the toilet and flushed it. I've called through, and Mr. Webb knows you're here, so he should only be a few minutes."

Carol thanked her warmly, then said, "Have you been at the school long?"

"Too right. Eleven years this December."

"I suppose you knew Dean Bayliss, then?"

Wendy's face became grave. "Poor Dean. That shouldn't happen to anyone, let alone him. I knew him right through from Year Seven, when he was a little boy. Bit of a follower, not a leader, but no harm in him."

Confidentially, Carol said, "We're still looking for a clear motive, so we're speaking with all his friends." She took out her notebook. "Would you mind checking this list to see if you could add anyone?"

Wendy looked closely at the names. "The principal's daughter, Caitlin, should be there. She went out with Dean until quite recently."

The principal's door opened, and a small boy with a wiry body and an angelic face came out. Webb followed him, saying to the back of his head, "You will be on afternoon detention for two weeks, Lachlan, and then I'll review the situation."

The small boy shot out his lower lip, rammed his hands in his pockets, and ambled off down the corridor.

Webb was wearing the same ill-fitting blue suit on his lanky body as the day before. "Come in, Inspector. I'm sorry to have kept you waiting."

Although his expression didn't change, he was not pleased at her request to see Eliot Donnovan. "I'm very reluctant to pull Eliot out of class. This is his final year, and every lesson is vital."

"I have his father's permission, but if you'd like to ring him . . ."

Webb tapped the tips of his stubby fingers together. "Very well." He picked up the phone. "I'll have him taken out of class and brought here. You can use my office, if you wish."

When he put down the receiver, Carol said, "I believe your daughter, Caitlin, was a close friend of Dean's. I'm a little surprised you didn't mention that yesterday."

Webb moved his small head from side to side as though his neck had suddenly become stiff. "I didn't say anything because, frankly, Caitlin has nothing to tell you, and I didn't want her disturbed."

With pleasant implacability, Carol said, "I would like to see Caitlin, as well as Eliot. Could you arrange it, please?"

"I'm sorry, that's not possible. My daughter isn't at school today. She's unwell."

"Perhaps I could call in to your house this evening?"

Webb took a deep breath. "I'm afraid she's too sick to see anyone. I'll contact you as soon as she's better."

He appeared to be relieved to hear a knock at the office door. Rising quickly, he said, "That will be Eliot. I'll leave you two alone."

Eliot Donnovan swaggered into the office and sat, knees wide apart, on a chair opposite Carol's. He was tall and wide shouldered, with high color and a self-indulgent mouth. His dark hair fell over his eyes, and he shoved it back. "What do you want?" he said.

Carol regarded him for a long moment, then took out her notebook and pretended to consult it. "We have information that you have recently been involved in vandalism on or near the Cosil-Ross property."

"What?" Taken by surprise, his cocky self-possession ebbed for a moment. He rallied to say combatively, "Who said that? It isn't true."

"Our reports indicate you were in the company of Scott Agar."

He straightened in his seat. "Is that what Scott says?"

Carol kept a look of polite inquiry on her face. "So you're denying it?"

"Of course I am! It's a lie."

Carol looked dubious. "When I interviewed Scott this morning about Dean Bayliss's murder..." She trailed off and waited for him to respond.

His former arrogance had been transformed into angry alarm. "What's Scott been saying about me?"

Carol consulted her notebook again. "I'm afraid I'm not at liberty to reveal anything specific from the interview."

"It was Bayliss," said Eliot. "Not me. Scott took Bayliss with him when they shot up the place."

"Indeed? Are you certain?"

Eliot scowled at her. "I'm certain."

Carol passed him the photograph of the medallion. "Do you recognize this?"

He turned it over in his fingers. "Didn't he tell you?" he said contemptuously. "This belonged to Scott. He gave it to his girlfriend, Becca Hamilton."

Bourke braked to let a tractor grind its way across the dirt road and enter the open gate of a plowed paddock. It was late afternoon, and long shadows zebra-striped the way. "When are you going to see the Hamilton girl again?"

"I've told Anne to speak with her," said Carol.

"Sort of a girlish heart-to-heart?" grinned Bourke.

"As soon as we get back, you can try the male version on Scott Agar. Eliot Donnovan will have called him by now with the happy news that we know about the medallion. It'll be interesting to see which way he goes — the truth or more lies."

The tractor finally jolted out of the way and Bourke accelerated with care on the slippery surface. "Rick Turner's sister isn't going to be pleased to see me again." He added mockingly, "I'd say she's down on all males at the moment. All hell will break loose when she tries for a property settlement with Stuart Cosil-Ross."

"I bet it will," said Carol, visualizing Elaine's unyielding manner, "especially if the sacred Cosil-Ross land is involved."

She would soon have an idea how much Stuart was worth. Working on the principle that ASIO would have the contacts and clout to access financial records with greater ease than the Police Service, Carol had asked Anne Newsome to make a covert contact with Denise Cleever and request urgent information on Elaine and Stuart Cosil-Ross, as well as Lizbeth Hamilton and Kent and Maggie Agar.

"I've passed on the information about the Volvo wagon to Sydney," said Bourke. When he had interviewed Rick Hunter's sister earlier that morning, she had been largely uncooperative, although she had identified the brown Volvo as being similar to a

141

vehicle with Queensland plates belonging to a strange man who'd called in to see her brother the week before.

Bourke turned off the road where a roughly painted sign nailed to a gum tree indicated the Turner property. A metal cattle grid vibrated under the wheels, then they were bumping along a muddy driveway. "Wait till you see the house," said Bourke, trying to avoid the deepest ruts. They jolted along for another ten minutes, then the farmhouse came into view.

It was a mean little building, unpainted and with a rusty metal roof. Several dilapidated sheds, leaning in imminent collapse, completed the depressing picture. A dog, heavily chained, barked savagely.

Bourke parked in the least muddy area near the front door, and they got out. Skirting puddles, they walked to the bottom of worn wooden steps, which had a disturbing cant to one side. "Here's the charming Hannah," Bourke murmured to Carol. "Don't be fooled by her sweet nature."

"What're you back here for?" demanded a woman in her early thirties who stood, hands on hips, on the narrow veranda. Her snug pink top, tight white jeans, and high-heeled black boots were distinctly out of place in the shabby, neglected setting.

Seemingly oblivious to her truculent glare, Bourke smiled up at her. "Inspector Ashton would like to ask you a few questions."

"I've said all I'm going to say."

Carol was willing to begin with civility. "Ms. Cosil-Ross —"

"I've dropped *that* name," she snapped. "I'm Hannah Turner."

"Ms. Turner ... We're very anxious to speak with your brother, and we're concerned that he seems to have disappeared."

Carol's mild approach was greeted with a ferocious scowl. "I know my rights. I don't have to talk to you. Now get the hell off the property."

Bourke said firmly, "Your brother may have come to some harm. This won't help him."

"Harm?" Hannah Turner said contemptuously. "Someone's put the wind up Rick and he's run for cover. That's more like it."

Hannah took an involuntary step back as Carol walked quickly up the stairs. Locking eyes with her, Carol said slowly and distinctly, "I'm investigating three murders. Yesterday, your local police sergeant was blown to pieces by a homemade bomb."

"Nothing to do with me."

Carol continued as though Hannah hadn't spoken, "There is every indication that your brother is involved in these murders, and if he is, this may make you an accomplice. Perhaps you already know that the law regards an accomplice as equally guilty of the crime."

"I don't have to talk to you," she repeated, but her voice was uncertain.

Carol shook her head regretfully. "I don't want to arrest you for hindering the investigation, but I will if I have to."

The pink sweater heaved in an impatient sigh. "Oh, all right. You'd better come in."

She led them through to the cramped kitchen, which, although shabby, was perfectly neat and clean. Flinging herself on a chair at the kitchen table, she waved ungraciously for them to be seated. "Hurry up.

I haven't got all day." She gave a disgusted grunt when Bourke took out his notebook. "This is a waste of time."

"You told Sergeant Bourke this morning that you saw Dean Bayliss on Saturday."

"He was here most of the day helping Rick." She rolled her eyes. "Like, they spent most of the time drinking beer."

"When did you last see Dean?"

Hannah gave Carol a long-suffering look. "I've already been through all this with *him.*" She glared at Bourke. "I told him I didn't know anything."

Waiting until Hannah's attention had swung back to her, Carol said, "Was it a lie when Becca Hamilton called on Saturday evening and you told her Dean and some of his friends were having a barbecue here?"

Hannah shrugged. "Rick and Dean went off in the late afternoon. Didn't say where they were going, but I got the idea they were meeting up with friends. When Dean's girlfriend rang up, I just wanted to get her off the phone. I mean, she was crying, and I'm way past listening to lovesick teenagers."

Carol questioned her about her brother's association with Dean Bayliss and his friends, but it was obvious that Hannah had no interest in the group. "I don't give a damn what Rick does. Believe me, I'd be out of this dump like a shot if I had the money."

"So the last time you saw him was Saturday afternoon?"

Obviously Hannah wasn't fretting about Rick Turner's disappearance. She snarled, "My bloody brother left me to deal with everyone who turned up on Sunday morning expecting to play games. They nearly drove me mad asking where Rick was and where the equipment was kept. I told them I'd call the cops if they didn't get lost."

"You weren't worried about your brother? You didn't think to report him missing?"

Carol's mild inquiry amused Hannah. "You're kidding me, right? Rick would hit the roof if he thought I'd tell the cops anything."

Carol took this opportunity to ask, "What did Rick think of Sergeant Griffin?"

She tossed her head impatiently. "I never asked him, but he was a cop, so Rick wouldn't like him on principle."

Bourke flipped a page of his notebook. "Why not?"

"Rick doesn't like anyone telling him what to do." She glinted at Carol. "And neither do I."

"Was there any particular reason why your brother resented the sergeant?"

"I told you, Rick thinks he's a big man around here."

"It seems to me," said Carol, "that the power in Katamulla is pretty well divided between the Cosil-Ross and the Agar families."

"That'd be about right," Hannah conceded, "though bloody Elaine wouldn't agree with you."

"You don't get on with your sister-in-law?"

Hannah gave a harsh laugh. "Get on with that bitch? No one could." Energized by antipathy, she sat forward in her chair. "Elaine made sure my marriage to Stuart never worked. She was against it from the very start, and I should have known better than to agree to live at the Grange." Her voice rose as she continued, "Stuart's a weakling. When push comes to shove, he always does what his sister tells him to do."

"She made things so unpleasant you had to leave?" Carol's tone was sympathetic.

Flushed with resentment and anger, Hannah said bitterly, "The thing that bloody gets me is that Elaine never minded having Rick around, it was only *me* she wanted to get rid of."

Bourke said, "Is there any hope of a reconciliation with your husband?"

"Not so long as that bitch is alive."

Carol didn't comment on Hannah's emphatic statement. Changing the subject, she said, "Your brother has been advertising what he calls fun war games in the *Recorder*."

Hannah sighed elaborately. "You come all this way to ask me about guys shooting paint at each other? I thought this was about murder."

"Could you tell us how he runs these games?" asked Bourke.

"Rick runs an ad and gets guys to come out to a spot in the bush about three kilometers from here. They pay him to rent the helmets, goggles, and paintball guns. Then he splits them into two teams and they go off into the bush and hunt each other. They spend hours crawling through the bush like little kids."

"Rick hasn't got a lot of money?"

Carol's question got a derisive snort from Hannah. "Take a look around. Rick hasn't got *any* money."

"Then how can he afford the equipment?"

"He didn't pay for it." She gave a bitter smile. "Bloody Elaine bankrolled him, didn't she?"

Later, bumping back along the neglected driveway, Bourke said, "If I were building up a militia group, I'd say paintball games would be ideal for recruiting."

"Appeal to the little boy playing soldier, you mean?" said Carol with a sideways grin. "Come on, admit it, Mark. You'd just *love* to get out there in camouflage and blaze away, wouldn't you?"

CHAPTER THIRTEEN

"Well here I am, Carol, following your written instructions." Madeline Shipley looked around the hotel dining room. "I didn't quite envisage this when I suggested we have dinner the other night."

"Good plain country cooking," said Carol. "You can't beat it."

It was early and the room was half empty, but those diners who were there were looking in their direction. This didn't surprise Carol. It wasn't just that Madeline Shipley was a prominent television personality who appeared on their screens night after night, but also that in person her beauty was incandescent. Her smooth skin, wide gray eyes, and assured smile were more arresting in reality than any electronic image could be.

"Sit down, Madeline, and stop causing a sensation."

Madeline acknowledged the interest in the room with a smile and a wave, then slid gracefully into the seat opposite Carol. "Well, Carol, I suppose I should be grateful you've fitted me into your busy schedule."

"It *is* busy. I'm sorry, Madeline, but this will have to be short."

Madeline gave her a hundred-watt smile. "Then I'd better talk fast. How about a date for a nightcap later? I'm flexible — your room or mine?"

"I'll have to take a rain check —"

"Of course you will, darling." Madeline's copper hair gleamed as she shook her head ruefully. "You're never easy, are you?"

The waitress, an angular young woman with acne whom Carol hadn't seen before, approached reverently. She handed them both menus, then fixed Madeline with a predatory stare. "Could I have your autograph, like?"

"Of course. Have you something I could sign?"

"Like, how about the menu? Would that be all right? You can use my pen."

Madeline smiled charmingly. "What's your name?"

"Diana. I spell it same as the princess."

She took the menu back delicately, checked what Madeline had written, said, "Gee, thanks," and put another one in front of her. "For Mum," she said. "Would you mind?" She twisted her head to see what Madeline was writing. "Her name's Opal."

149

Satisfied, she gave Madeline a fresh menu from which to order, then hovered until they made their selections.

"It's the price of fame," said Madeline with a laugh as Diana retreated, autographed menus firmly under one arm. She lowered her voice to say, "And speaking of fame, I was flattered to have a visit from a certain Mr. Trevorwill before I left Sydney this morning." She put up a hand at Carol's frown. "I'm not saying another word, darling, but I *do* expect to have an exclusive from you when you can talk. That isn't too much to ask, is it?"

"You always push it, don't you?" said Carol.

"I do." Madeline was complacent. "And you'd hate me any other way."

When Carol pushed open the swing doors, a blast of noise and hot air hit her face. The bar of the Katamulla pub was rapidly filling with patrons intent on a good time, as well as a sprinkling of reporters who would later justify their presence as gathering local color. A television set bleated overhead, smoke and conversation swelled. Beryl and Herb Bennett, accompanied by a barman with an open, freckled face, labored to fill shouted orders.

The long bar still had a brass footrest running its full length, testament to the past when male drinkers had lounged, one elbow on the bar, to chugalug their schooners of beer. Times had changed. High stools lined the bar. The rest of the available space was jammed with tables and chairs and two billiard tables.

"Carol. Over here." Bourke waved from a table in one corner. Carol threaded her way through the narrow spaces between chairs as Bourke appropriated a chair from another table. "Here, squeeze in at the end."

He grinned at her. "Let me introduce you . . ." He indicated the two women at the table. "Denise North and Gwen Pickard — we've just met. And Ned Millet and Doug Rush, borrowed from the Harmerville cops." Bourke made a sweeping gesture in Carol's direction. "Meet my boss, Carol Ashton."

"We met at the school, I think," said Carol to Gwen Pickard, who was sucking hard on a cigarette.

She nodded pleasantly to Denise, diverted to see that she had abandoned her glasses, had put on copious makeup, and was wearing a demure pastel pink blouse and deeper pink skirt.

She turned her attention to the two constables who had been allocated to her team. They had been working under Bourke's supervision, tracing Griffin's movements and checking the police station files for any possible motives for the bombing.

Ned Millet had soot-black hair and a thin nose that was set like a knife blade on his prematurely-lined face. His long fingers played with his beer glass, and his eyes slid away from Carol when she smiled at him.

The other constable, Doug Rush, was a chunky young man whose biceps strained the sleeves of his sports shirt. From the thickness of his short neck and the bulk of his shoulders, Carol guessed that he was a dedicated body builder.

Bourke ordered a repeat round of drinks and a scotch on the rocks for Carol. "Denise is staying here at the hotel. She's a book traveler, or something."

"Representative," said Denise with a giggle. "I'm here to open up the territory for textbooks, mainly." She looked brightly around the table. "I met Gwen at the school this afternoon, and she was kind enough to suggest we have a drink together." Denise gave Doug Rush a hopeful smile. "Gwen says the pub's the best place to meet people."

Carol joined in the inconsequential conversation at the table, raising her voice to be heard above the decibels generated by other patrons' alcohol-fueled merriment. Gwen Pickard had a keen sense of humor and told diverting stories about school, her pale eyes squinting through the smoke of the cigarettes she chain-smoked.

Doug Rush, Carol decided after a few minutes, was a stultifyingly dull young man, who seemed to have no topics of conversation other than the relative merits of different cars and trucks. Ned Millet was more interesting, if only for the fact that he was an enigma, who said not one thing even remotely personal, but freely discussed any subject raised in a knowledgeable way.

Watching Denise perform, Carol had to admit that she was a competent actor, playing the part of a sweet, rather naive woman who was keen to attract male company. Carol had to remind herself that Gwen Pickard was acting too, although in her case she didn't have to stretch to take on a totally unfamiliar career.

After about half an hour, Gwen Pickard excused herself, saying she had essays to mark. Twenty minutes later, Denise, artlessly showing her disappointment that none of the males at the table seemed particularly interested in her, announced that she was tired and was going to have an early night.

Denise's chair was hard against the wall, so everyone at the table was forced to rise so that she could get out. Denise took advantage of the situation to hiss into Carol's ear, "Room eighteen in fifteen minutes."

Glad to have an excuse to get out of the cacophony, Carol waited twelve minutes, then said she had to call Sydney.

There was no one in the entrance foyer. She walked quickly up the stairs, found room eighteen, and tapped lightly on the door.

Denise opened the door just enough to let her in. Closing it behind her, Denise said, "Jeez! That was the pits! If I'd had to give one more girlish giggle, I'd have thrown up."

Carol was diverted to see that the theme of Denise's room was brown. The carpeting was a rich chocolate, the walls beige, and Gwen Pickard was perched on a tan bedspread. From the evidence of the ashtray on the side table, she had already had two cigarettes. Lighting up her third, she took a deep draw, then said through the exhaled stream of smoke, "You certainly stirred things up at school this afternoon, Inspector."

"I did?"

Denise interpreted Carol's quick glance around the room. "It's safe to talk, Carol. The room's been swept for electronic devices. It's clean. So's yours, by the way."

"What happened?" said Carol.

Gwen ran a hand through her frizzy hair. "You had Eliot Donnovan pulled out of my English class. When he came back he was pretty off the wall. He whispered to a couple of his mates at the back of the room — naturally he's the sort who always sits as far away from the teacher as possible — and then he got up, told me he had to go, and walked out." She paused to take another substantial nicotine hit. "And then I found out that Webb had a meeting scheduled with some heavy from the Education Department, but he called it off at the last moment and left in a big hurry. *Very* uncharacteristic — he usually shamelessly kisses up to authority."

Denise, leaning negligently against the wall, said mockingly, "Just what *did* you do, Carol?"

Carol briefly summarized the two conversations. Gwen nodded when she mentioned Caitlin Webb. "I'm not surprised he wasn't keen to have you asking questions about his daughter. The word is she had an abortion, and the father was Dean Bayliss. Webb's such a self-righteous shit, he'd rather die than let on his beloved daughter got herself pregnant."

Denise said, "Gwen may have a lead on Ken Kirk."

"You know where he is?" Although the constable's mother had said vaguely that he was staying with friends, a quick check during the day had turned up no leads.

Stubbing out her cigarette, Gwen said, "I've got an idea why he disappeared. A friend of Kirk's mother works at the school canteen, and she says Kirk got a letter in the mail earlier in the week that frightened the hell out of him. Something about how he'd been found guilty and would be punished."

"The people's court strikes again," said Denise. "No wonder he bolted after he saw firsthand what could happen."

Gwen coughed, a thick, phlegmy sound. "There's more," she said, "I hear that Kirk told his mother that something dreadful was going to happen, Australia-wide. He didn't give any details, but Mrs. Kirk told her friend that he was terribly upset."

"Any time frame?"

"No."

Denise said, "We need to get Kirk and find out exactly what he knows. Fortunately we might just have a lead."

"Here's an address," said Gwen, handing Carol a piece of paper. "It's an ex-girlfriend of Ken Kirk's who lives in Liverpool, outside Sydney. Wouldn't be surprised if that's where he is."

"If he's there, we'll have him picked up."

"We've been watching Kent Agar," said Denise. "Like Constable Kirk, he seems to be terrified. He's canceled his visit here as the VIP for the bushranger thing, and he's hired a bodyguard. His wife's ordered him home, but he's digging in his heels."

"ASIO is tapping the phone?"

Denise grinned. "Quite legally, I must assure you."

"Who has he called in Katamulla?"

Denise consulted a folder. "Elaine Cosil-Ross for

one. That was a short, sharp conversation, as she wasn't a bit pleased he was bailing out of the weekend celebrations. Straight after that he rang the *Recorder* to ask the editor to put a positive spin on the fact he wouldn't be in Katamulla as guest of honor on Saturday. He also spoke to Donnovan's hardware store to order some things to be sent out to his house. And he called the pub here to dispute a liquor account. That's about it, except for his wife. She called him this afternoon."

"After I'd been there?"

"You do have a way of upsetting people," said Denise. "Agar and his wife had a very acrimonious conversation after you left the house. Kent wasn't at all pleased that Maggie Agar allowed you through the door, and she wasn't impressed with his criticism, so she gave it to him with both barrels."

Denise smiled reminiscently. "The kindest thing she said to her husband was that he was a spineless weakling who caved in when the going got rough."

"Did she mention the Saint Christopher's medallion?"

"That's the only point that Kent and Maggie agreed upon — that everyone in the family should deny ever knowing anything about it. Surprisingly enough, it seems that Eliot Donnovan told you the truth this afternoon. Scott Agar did give this particular family heirloom to Becca Hamilton as a token of his love. He and Dean Bayliss were certainly rivals, although Dean appeared to have the edge."

Carol regarded her with a cynical smile. "Is ASIO tapping any other phones?"

"Not a one," said Denise righteously. "But I wouldn't tell my deepest secrets if I were using a cellular phone in the area — we're scanning the mobile frequencies twenty-four hours a day."

Checking her watch, Carol said, "I've got a meeting scheduled with Mark and Anne Newsome. I'll get back to you if there's anything you should know." She hesitated at the door. "When can I expect the financial information I asked for?"

"Tomorrow afternoon at the earliest." Denise added dryly, "Financial institutions just hate cooperating — it's a bloody sight easier to get permission to tap a phone than to find out the most minor detail about someone's money."

Before she opened the door, Denise said sharply, "You're armed, aren't you?"

"Of course."

"It's just," Denise patted her shoulder, "I'd really hate anything to happen to you, Carol."

Grinning to herself because she felt rather like a character in a French farce, Carol slipped along the corridor and tapped on Bourke's door. "A symphony in blue," he said, indicating the furnishings. "You say you're yellow, I'm blue, and poor Anne is a particularly bilious green."

"My room's better with the light out," Anne laughed. "Otherwise the green walls sort of sway in toward me."

Carol took the proffered chair, which featured an embroidered cobalt cushion. Handing Bourke the address Gwen Pickard had given her, she said, "Ken Kirk may be here. It's the address of an ex-girlfriend of his. If he is there, I want him brought back here under guard, and no one is to interview him before we do."

"Don't ask me about Scott and the heirloom

medallion," said Bourke, "because I've got bugger-all. When I called Maggie Agar to say we needed to ask a few more questions, she said very emphatically that Scott wasn't available. I pushed as hard as I could, and she said she'd get back to me. I'm not holding my breath."

"What about the files at the station? Anything of interest in them?"

"Certainly no cases that would cause someone to construct a bomb. The vandalism Elaine Cosil-Ross complained about was noted, but there were no names of suspects in the file."

"I suppose there wasn't a mention of Inner Circle or any militia activity."

"Nothing." He handed her a sheet of paper. "But I have got something about Arnie Griffin's last day on earth." He leaned over her shoulder as she looked at the page. "Since Ken Kirk has skipped and so many documents were destroyed in the explosion, Millet and Rush had to get most of the information from a log in Griffin's car. You can see a lot is routine stuff. Griffin called in on a guy whose dog ate a neighbor's chickens, spoke to someone else who's been playing loud music at two in the morning, and spent some time at the town hall discussing crowd control for this weekend's festivities. He also had a note to himself to call in at the pub."

He pointed halfway down the page. "Now these later items may be more interesting: Griffin sees the Bayliss family; calls into the bakery where Dean worked; drives out to the Cosil-Ross place."

Frowning over the list, Carol said, "On one of these stops he was given a parcel bomb."

"Not necessarily," said Bourke. "He could have been carrying it around for days. Or when he was walking out of the town hall, someone could have handed it to him."

"It must have been someone he trusted," said Anne. "After all, he'd just got a letter threatening him, so ˄ he wouldn't be taking anything suspicious from strangers."

"And it was something he didn't open until he got back to the station." Bourke blew out his cheeks. "A gift of some sort?" He pondered. "I know it wasn't his birthday, but perhaps an anniversary ... ?"

"It's worth checking out."

Anne Newsome said quickly, "I've got an idea about it."

Anne had been leaning against the black-metal bed end, but now she was on the balls of her feet, her olive skin flushed. Carol thought that the young constable was like a bloodhound about to be loosed, so keen that she was almost quivering.

"I got nothing much from the teachers who gave you their names yesterday, *except* ..." Anne paused for maximum drama, "... the school librarian. Sergeant Griffin was the president of the local historical society, and she's been working with him on a big display for Bushranger Week."

"So?" said Bourke.

"So they've been collecting photos, documents, and artifacts from all the old families for the exhibition." Anne flung her hands wide. "It was Sergeant Griffin who was collecting them. Wouldn't you think that valuable things like that would be wrapped when people gave them to him?"

Bourke nodded slowly. "And the two oldest families are the Agars and the Cosil-Rosses. No doubt they both contributed material."

"That's a good angle, Anne," said Carol, gently amused when the young constable was so obviously pleased with the praise. "Follow it up tomorrow."

"And I've seen Becca Hamilton," said Anne. "I'm sure she recognized the Saint Christopher, but she said she'd never seen it before." She grimaced, obviously annoyed with herself. "I tried being friendly; I tried being tough. But even when I said that Eliot Donnovan had identified it as being the one Scott gave her, she said she couldn't remember getting it. Then her mother came in and made it clear she thought I was harassing her daughter."

"The parents around here are a protective lot," said Bourke.

"Maybe they've got a lot to hide," said Anne.

CHAPTER FOURTEEN

Waking early with a severe crick in her back, Carol tried to find a comfortable position on the sagging mattress while she reviewed the day ahead. She expected to hear this morning if Constable Kirk had been located, and if so, she wanted to interview him as soon as possible. In the meantime, she would send Anne around to see his mother to confirm that he had received an anonymous letter. Carol was curious to know if there had been a yellow circle in the envelope.

The two constables, Rush and Millet, could check

with the school librarian and compile a list of those in the district who had offered to provide material for the historical display.

She and Bourke would interview Scott Agar and Becca Hamilton. And then Caitlin Webb, the principal's daughter.

Carol got out of bed, her toes curling on the cold floor. After all the food she had eaten the day before, she was determined to have a good workout. She dressed in a blue tracksuit and laced up her running shoes.

She considered the guns. The Beretta was too heavy, and not only would the ankle holster of the Glock 27 not fit under her tight pants, the gun's weight would throw out her stride. After a moment's thought she put the Beretta and the briefing files in an overnight bag and stuffed the subcompact Glock into the right-hand zipper pocket of her top. It was small, but its bulk would still bump against her ribs as she ran.

On the way out she stopped at Anne Newsome's door with the overnight bag. When Anne, fully dressed, answered her knock, Carol asked her to keep an eye on the bag until she got back.

Outside, the air was frosty and the street deserted. She did a few stretching exercises — always less than recommended, she knew — and set off down the main street, jogging past the churches and the Imperial Cafe, which was the only point of activity, with puffs of steam rising above the kitchen where breakfast was being cooked.

Carol turned left and ran down toward the river.

She'd driven over a fine stone bridge yesterday, and she wanted to look at it more closely. A strip of parkland edged the river at this point, so Carol deviated from the road to run along a paved path that wound between landscaped bushes.

The sun had risen above the horizon, staining the clouds with red. Carol breathed deeply, the comfort of her rhythmic steps rising up through her body to calm her thoughts.

Ahead she saw another runner coming toward her along the path. Carol automatically categorized him: male, medium height, wide shoulders, sturdy build, brown curly hair, regular features, wearing a black Nike tracksuit.

He jogged past her, raising a friendly hand in greeting. She didn't look back, until the steady slap of his running shoes changed tempo.

She turned quickly, but he was upon her. The short length of pipe in his right hand glinted dully as he swung it viciously at her head. She instinctively put up her arm as a shield, and the blow hit her elbow.

The pain was a numbing agony that paralyzed her right arm. She stumbled, regained her balance, stingingly aware that there was no way she could get her gun out.

His left arm outstretched, his right raised above his head with his weapon, the man thrust his contorted face at her. "You have been judged and found guilty!"

He used his left hand to backhand her across the face, then seized her useless arm and swung her

163

toward him. "The people's court has passed sentence." Spittle splashed her face. "This is your just punishment!"

As she pulled away, he swung the pipe in an arc, striking her ribs a glancing blow.

There was no time for fear or anger. The techniques she had practiced until they were automatic came into play.

As he pulled at her arm, Carol stopped resisting. She transferred her weight to her front foot, the heel of her left hand punching forward in a short, jolting blow under his jaw. His head snapped back, but he didn't release her.

"Cunt!"

She relaxed, then lashed out with a chopping blow at eye level that caught him on the bridge of the nose.

He gave a howl of pain, releasing her to clutch at his face. The hand holding the length of pipe fell to his side.

Carol balanced herself and leaned away from her attacker, shifting all her weight to her left leg. She drew her right leg up, her knee angled towards her left shoulder. With all her power she struck downward at his left knee joint.

There was a sharp crack as bone snapped. Even as he shrieked and fell writhing to the ground she was ready for another blow.

Carol kicked the length of pipe out of his reach, and then stood panting, cradling her injured elbow. "Try to get up," she ground out, "and I'll break the other one."

* * * * *

164

"Inspector Ashton, I heard you'd been physically attacked..." Elaine Cosil-Ross, her patrician face concerned, stood at the doorway of a small parlor Carol had temporarily appropriated at the hotel. She was impeccably turned out in a tweed jacket and skirt, with a single strand of pearls at the neck of her silk blouse.

"Nothing serious. I've a bruised elbow and a cut lip, that's all." Carol rose from the table she had improvised as a desk. "Can I help you with something?"

"I'm here for last-minute arrangements for the parade, of course, but when I heard that you had been hurt, I felt I should call to see you. Things like this just don't happen in Katamulla. I do hope you won't judge us by this one incident." She paused to inspect Carol's face. "You've got a nasty graze there. Has anyone been apprehended?"

This last question, Carol thought, was almost certainly the reason Elaine Cosil-Ross was there. "He's in the hospital, at the moment, with a police guard. I've no idea if he's a local man, as yet."

"In the hospital?" Elaine raised her eyebrows. "Am I to take it you shot him, Inspector?"

"No. I just got in a lucky blow."

"Inspector Ashton's too modest," said Herb Bennett. He slid the tray with coffee and biscuits onto the table. "She broke the lout's knee." He nodded respectfully to Elaine. "May I get you anything, Ms. Cosil-Ross?"

"No, nothing, thanks. I must be going."

After Elaine Cosil-Ross left, Herb Bennett continued to stand by Carol's chair. "Yes?" she said. "Is there something...?"

He rubbed his big-knuckled hands together. "I was wondering... I know the Bayliss family well, and Dean was a good boy..." He moved restlessly. "Well, I'd like to know whoever did that to him was going to come to justice. What I'm saying is that I'd feel better if I thought you were making progress, if you know what I mean."

"Mr. Bennett, I'm afraid —"

He put up a big hand to forestall her. "I understand. I shouldn't have asked." He gave an embarrassed half-laugh. "It's Beryl, you see. She likes to know what's going on."

Carol gazed thoughtfully at his retreating back, then returned to the papers in front of her. Denise had been too cynical — the financial reports had arrived that morning by security courier.

Stuart Cosil-Ross's boast of family wealth had not been an empty one. The fortune the first members of the family had amassed had grown steadily over the years so that both brother and sister, apart from the value of their jointly-owned farming property, were individually extremely rich. There was a note that Elaine Cosil-Ross contributed generously to a North American think tank renowned for its right-wing extremist views, and also to its Australian counterpart. Both she and her brother had provided considerable funds to Kent Agar's election campaigns over the years.

Carol turned to Kent Agar's records with interest, but there was nothing suspicious about his finances. In her own right Maggie Agar was well off, having inherited money, and it was apparent she had entirely financed the white monstrosity that had replaced Kent Agar's family home.

Lizbeth Hamilton hadn't been paid a cent for her husband's death. The money to modernize the newspaper had been given to her in the form of a no-interest loan from Elaine Cosil-Ross.

Bourke came in as she was finishing the documents. He carefully shut the door before he said, "The guy who attacked you isn't saying anything, but we know who he is from his fingerprints." He grinned. "The wonders of modern science really work when you've got ASIO on your side."

"He's not a local?"

"Queenslander. Name's Shadworth. He's got a couple of assault convictions in Brisbane, but the most interesting thing about him is that he's the registered owner of a Volvo station wagon. A brown one. We haven't located it yet, but I'll bet it's somewhere in the district."

"I want to see him."

Bourke shook his head. "Too late, Carol. He's on his way to Harmerville under guard. Denise said to tell you she'd keep you informed of his interrogation."

Carol indicated the financial records. "There's nothing here, except that the Cosil-Rosses support right-wing causes — and that's no crime." She slumped back in the chair.

Bourke looked at her with concern. "How are you feeling?"

Not wanting to admit that she felt a little shaky, Carol grinned at him. "A lot better than the other guy."

"Well enough to come to the station? After Ken Kirk was picked up early this morning at his girlfriend's place, I arranged for him to be brought here as quickly as possible. They've just arrived."

Gathering her things together, Carol said, "After we finish questioning Kirk, I want him held in solitary at Harmerville — I don't care what the charge is."

"Protective custody?" said Bourke. "I reckon he'll need it."

Temporary repairs had been done to the front of the station building, but the office had been relocated at the back. Carol told the two officers who had escorted the constable from Liverpool to have a break and seated herself opposite Kirk. Bourke stood, hands in pockets.

Ken Kirk was unshaven and frightened. His prominent Adam's apple kept bobbing as he swallowed nervously, and he couldn't keep his fingers still.

He stared at Carol as though she were an avenging angel. "It wasn't my fault. I couldn't have stopped it. They would have got the Sarge, no matter what."

"Who would have got him?" Bourke inquired.

He glanced at Bourke, then back to Carol. "You know, don't you?"

Carol narrowed her eyes. "We need a name,

Constable," she said with deliberate impatience. "You're going to tell us everything you know."

He licked his lips. "They'll kill me."

"Look, Kirk," Bourke said wearily, "you're small fry. They're not going to bother about you." He leaned forward to shove his face into the constable's. "But *we* are. I reckon we could charge you with being an accessory to Sergeant Griffin's death, and make it stick."

"Inner Circle," mumbled Kirk, his head down.

"Say it again."

Kirk looked up. "They call themselves Inner Circle. I heard about it from Rick Turner. He's a real bullshit artist, so I didn't really believe him when he told me the Sarge was going to be taught a lesson." His face screwed up with misery. "Jesus, I never thought . . ."

Carol said, "Apart from Rick Turner, do you know any specific names?"

Kirk shook his head violently. "No names." He swallowed. "But I know they're everywhere."

"Everywhere? What does that mean?"

Kirk didn't answer Bourke's question. Burying his head in his hands, he said, "They're going to kill me, I know they are."

After arranging for Kirk to be held in protective custody in Harmerville, Bourke dropped Carol back at her hotel. A rehearsal for the parade was in full swing, so he had to let her out on a side street. She walked up to the main thoroughfare and joined the crowd in front of the pub, being careful to protect her bruised elbow from the enthusiasm of fellow spectators.

The Katamulla High School band, resplendent in blue uniforms and gold braid, were marching past, almost in step. They were playing "Waltzing Matilda" with more enthusiasm than accuracy, but everyone applauded loudly anyway.

Over the noise a voice said in Carol's ear, "Inspector, I must speak with you on an important matter."

Turning to see Maggie Agar, Carol gestured toward the hotel entrance. The foyer was deserted. Carol led her to the small parlor. "We can talk in here."

There was an urgency about Maggie Agar today that had been entirely missing at Carol's first meeting with her. Carol motioned for her to sit down, but she refused.

Her soft voice tremulous, she said, "I have to confess I wasn't entirely frank with you the other day."

Carol made it easy for her. "About the medallion? We know it's a family heirloom of yours."

Maggie Agar bit her lip. "It wasn't Scott's fault, he knew I wanted him to lie. I wouldn't want him to be in trouble."

"Sergeant Bourke will be interviewing Scott again today." Carol was matter-of-fact. "As long as your son answers his questions truthfully, there won't be any problem."

"He can't interview Scott today," said Maggie Agar, twisting her hands together. "That's why I've come to you. I don't know where Scott is."

"You think he's come to some harm?"

She blinked rapidly. "Kent told me not to bother you, that Scott's gone off with friends . . ."

"What do you think?"

"I'm sure something's wrong." Maggie Agar's mouth hardened. "Scott would never dare to leave without telling me *exactly* where he was going."

"Poor baby," cooed Madeline. "It was very wise of you to agree to an early night. You need some comforting."

"I'm fine. Just a bit stiff."

Madeline grinned wickedly. "I could massage those stiff points, darling."

Carol's reluctant smile caused a twinge of pain in her bruised jaw. "You're just trying to take advantage of my weakened state."

"I sure am!" Madeline opened the door, bent down to get something from the floor outside in the hall, and turned around with a tray bearing an ice bucket, a bottle of black label Johnnie Walker, and two fat tumblers. "Voila!" she said triumphantly as she shut the door with her hip. "Medicinal alcohol to take the edge off your agony."

She glanced over at the French doors leading to the veranda that ran the full length of the hotel. "Now, what I have in mind for you demands privacy." Setting down the tray on the bedside table, she strode over to check the lock.

In spite of the discomfort of her bruises, while she watched Madeline pulling down the two yellow vinyl roller blinds to cover the glass, Carol felt a tickle of desire.

There was a perverse thrill in surrendering for a moment. Madeline was in charge, sure of herself. Carol said lightly, "I'm just humoring you, you know. I'll leap up in a moment and throw you out of the room."

Madeline handed her a tumbler. "Scotch on the rocks, and I hope you note I've gone for the best the hotel can provide."

They clinked glasses. "To us," said Madeline.

The bedside lamp shone through the amber liquid. Carol took a mouthful and held it for a moment before swallowing. It stung the cut at the corner of her mouth and then traced a warm path to her stomach. She sighed, "That was good."

"You ain't seen nothing yet."

"Madeline," she said with a grin that changed to a grimace of pain, "whatever you have in mind, you'll have to be gentle with me."

"I'll have to examine you closely," said Madeline as she opened the front of Carol's robe. She bent to gently kiss each nipple. "Hey, playing doctors is fun!"

Her smile faded as she took in the dark bruising along Carol's ribs. "The bastard. I hope you hit him bloody hard."

It was strange, and exciting, to see the usually impatient Madeline take so much time and care. She slowly eased the robe away from Carol's shoulders, kissing her gently and running her fingers softly over bare skin.

Then she undressed, equally slowly, her gray eyes intent on Carol the whole time.

Sliding onto the bed beside her she purred, "Are you feeling better?"

"Maybe."

"I'll make sure you feel *much* better. Probably better than you can bear."

"Promises," said Carol.

Madeline began an unrelentingly gentle pressure. "Don't move darling, just lie there and leave everything to me."

Carol's hips jerked, her head went back. Dimly she was aware of her injuries, her swollen elbow bumping against Madeline's smooth body, but all this, the glow of the lamp, Madeline's low, soothing voice, the taste of Madeline in her mouth, all receded until she was pure feeling, flying free.

Gasping, she was brought to earth by her body's jolting delight. "Darling?" Carol said.

"Just relax. Go to sleep. I'll stay here with you," said Madeline, "just like Florence Nightingale." She gave a low chuckle. "That woman *did* like the company of woman, didn't she?"

CHAPTER FIFTEEN

Saturday was clear and cold and sunny, a beautiful winter day and perfect for the launch of Bushranger Week.

Carol left Madeline curled like a sleepy kitten and put on jeans, a sweater, and a denim jacket to conceal her Beretta nine-millimeter. Wincing from her bruises, she strapped the Glock's holster to her right ankle, thinking how stupidly overconfident she had been the morning before, just because she had been carrying the Glock in her zippered pocket. She'd been told many times by firearms instructors that a gun was a useless defense in an emergency unless it was immediately accessible, and yesterday had been a textbook example of this.

She decided to walk down to the Imperial Cafe and have breakfast, so she slid some money into the back pocket of her jeans and left her bag locked in a suitcase.

Early though it was, final preparations for the parade were already underway. The motorized float depicting a tableau of Doom O'Reilly's final confrontation with the state troopers was in place, and prefabricated stands for VIPs were being assembled outside the town hall.

As she neared the Imperial Cafe, Constable Rush pulled beside the curb in a patrol car. "We've got Rick Turner!" He leaned over and opened the passenger side door. "He's at the station. I'll give you a lift."

Carol got into the patrol car, shoving an empty polystyrene coffee cup and food wrappings onto the floor.

"Sorry about that," said Doug Rush. "Meant to clean it up." He looked over his shoulder and pulled carefully out into the light traffic. "I left Millet calling you and Sergeant Bourke, and went out for breakfast. I was on my way back when I saw you."

"How did you get Turner?"

"Millet and I were on early duty. Turner just came in to the station and said he'd heard we were looking for him."

Carol glanced over at the constable. His thick neck strained at the collar of his uniform, and his flushed cheeks and animated manner showed an agitated excitement. She asked if Rick Turner had said anything about where he had been for the past week.

"We've haven't questioned him at all. We were waiting for you, Inspector."

Rush turned into the police station parking area and drew to a stop. As the constable reached down beside the driver's seat, Carol looked around, alert to the fact that there were no other vehicles in the lot. The hairs on her neck prickled, and she made a grab for the gun in her shoulder holster.

"Don't!" Rush had his service revolver leveled at her. He jammed it hard into her side. "Both hands out where I can see them."

She didn't obey him. The tips of her fingers were touching the cool metal of the Beretta. Calculating the odds, Carol stared into his eyes. "This is a mistake, Doug. Put the gun down, and we'll talk it out."

"No way!" Sweat was pouring down his face, and he was shaking so violently that the barrel of his revolver was bumping against her ribs. "Rick? Where the fuck are you?" he called.

The car's back door opened and a man slid in behind Carol. "Right here. Stop shouting, you stupid prick."

The man put his arm around the side of the seat until his hand was across her throat. Pulling her head back roughly against the headrest, he said, "See this, bitch? It's a forty-four Magnum with hollow-point ammunition. It'll blow your head away, so don't even think of going for your gun."

Doug Rush opened her jacket and pulled out Carol's Beretta. "Got it!"

"Give it to me, then check her out — she might be carrying something else."

As the constable, still shaking, clumsily fumbled in Carol's pockets, the man in back snarled, "Hurry up. We've got to get out of here."

He tightened his grip on her throat until she gagged. "Shut up, bitch."

Carol turned her right foot so that the little Glock holstered on her ankle was pressed against the front of the seat. Rush, awkwardly bent in the confined space, was sloppy in his search, cursorily running his hands over her jeans.

"She's clean."

"Then drive!" He poked the barrel of his gun under the point of Carol's jaw. "Just sit there and enjoy the ride. If you try anything, it'll be the last thing you do."

As the car picked up speed, Carol assessed her situation. The traffic was light, and they were taking back roads leading directly into the countryside. Madeline would assume she had been called away because of some development in the case, and even when the alarm was raised, it was highly unlikely that anyone who might have noticed her get into the patrol car would remember the incident.

The man in the back said to Rush, "Call in on the mobile and say we've got her. The Commander will be waiting to hear."

Rush reached into the side pocket of the door and took out a cellular phone. Juggling with the steering wheel, he pulled up the aerial and punched in the key for an code for an automatically-dialed number. He held it to his left ear, and Carol could hear the tinny sound of the ring. There was a click as the phone was answered. Rush said, "It went to plan. The goods are safe. We're on our way now." He didn't wait for any response before cutting the connection.

Carol assumed that the man behind her holding the Magnum to the side of her neck was Rick Turner. He still had his hand hard against her throat so there was no way she could lean down and grab her little gun. Small though it was, it held nine point-forty-caliber rounds and an additional one in the chamber. That would give her ten shots, if she ever had the opportunity to use it.

"You're Rick Turner, aren't you? I spoke with your sister." It was standard negotiating practice to try to form some sort of personal relationship with hostage-takers, and to use their names whenever possible. "She seemed to be worried about you, Rick."

He made a derisive sound. "Hannah never gives a fuck about anyone but herself." He tightened his grip on Carol's throat. "Shut up. I'm not in a talkative mood."

Carol glanced sideways at Doug Rush. His hands were gripping the wheel so tightly the knuckles showed white and the muscles were bunched in his jaw. "Where are we going, Doug?"

Rush turned his head and Carol realized that he was both scared and elated. "Rick told you to shut up."

He was the weak point. Carol said regretfully, "The longer this goes on, the worse it gets for you, Doug. You can still get out of it okay — it isn't too late."

Her ears rang as Rick Turner clubbed her across the side of the head with the Magnum. "No more talk, or I'll really lay into you."

Carol sat silent. She was sure they were members of Inner Circle, and she had no illusions that they intended to leave her alive. She tried to relax, to conserve her strength. Realistically, there was no point in trying anything in the car, particularly with Rick Turner behind her in the backseat. They believed she was unarmed, and there might be some opportunity when they got to their destination.

She recognized a turnoff and realized they were heading toward the Cosil-Ross property. They didn't slow at the main gate to the Grange, however, but continued along the road for several kilometers.

Turner said from the backseat, "Call in and say we'll be there in twenty minutes." He sniggered. "I'm sure there'll be a welcoming committee."

Rush obediently retrieved the cell phone and punched the automatic dial function. "Twenty minutes," he said. "We've got our passenger secure, and we're not far from the top gate."

"Have a good look around, bitch," said Turner. "You won't be seeing it again." He poked the Magnum's barrel into the hollow below her ear. "Want to know what's going to happen to you? Are you going to blubber and scream like Bayliss?"

"You were part of the firing squad?"

Carol's cool question seemed to amuse Constable Rush. "You could say Rick was *there*," he chortled, "but he's such a lousy shot I reckon he didn't hit anywhere near the target."

"Shut the fuck up," Turner snarled at him.

Anger was always a distraction. Hoping to needle him, Carol said to Turner, "You were using a twenty-two. Right?"

"Girls' gun," said Rush, as he slowed and turned onto a graded dirt surface, stopping at a heavily-padlocked gate that spanned the road.

As Rush got out to open it, Carol tensed. Rick Turner hissed, "Don't even think of it."

Rush drove through, then went back to secure the gate. Carol looked around. As far as she could remember from the map she had studied, they were at the western end of the Cosil-Ross valley where the original farmhouse had been built.

They started off again, the well-cared-for road leading in a series of gentle loops down into the valley through land that had obviously never been cleared. Thick vegetation crowded the road, and through it Carol caught glimpses of towering sandstone cliffs.

"Real wild country here," said Rick Turner with relish. "You could die and never be found."

Iron roofs came into view below them. The road, dropping gradually, curved gracefully as it reached the floor of the valley. Carol was taut, memorizing everything she saw. If she were to escape, she needed to have a clear concept of where things were in relationship to each other. She visualized looking at the map on the wall of the parlor and Stuart Cosil-Ross pointing out different items to her.

This original homestead, built on the same pattern of wide verandas as the newer one, was not nearly as grand but was still a substantial size.

Beside it was the square ugliness of an obviously new corrugated-iron building with huge double doors.

There was a welcoming committee. Several men and women wearing camouflage military fatigues stood waiting. She recognized two of them. The first was Scott Agar, who smirked at her triumphantly. The second was the man who strode forward, his gut straining against the khaki and green pattern of his uniform. "Get out of the car," barked Herb Bennett, "and put your hands behind your neck."

She got her first good look at Rick Turner when he followed her out of the car. He was short and sinewy, with lank greasy hair and a loose, thick-lipped mouth. He grinned widely at her. "Feeling frightened, bitch? You should be."

"That's enough," Bennett said to him.

As soon as they were out of the vehicle, Doug Rush turned it around and began to drive back the way they had come.

"He's going off to send your mates off on a wild-goose chase." Turner's tone was malicious. "We've arranged for Millet to get a tip from a guy he trusts that you're being taken out of the district, and Rush will turn up with the same information."

Herb Bennett stared coldly. "You talk too much, Turner."

A party of five — two men and three women — marched Carol around the side of the farmhouse past several trucks and four-wheel drives. Near the back door three huts made of concrete blocks had been constructed in the area that had once been the vegetable garden. Carol was pushed inside the nearest hut, and the metal door was slammed behind her. She heard the rattle of a padlock being inserted in the hasp and locked shut.

Light came from a series of narrow gaps left between the concrete blocks of the top tier, directly under the flat metal roofing. There was a mattress on the floor, a folded gray blanket, and an old ice cream container full of water. Otherwise the cell was bare.

After examining everything in the cramped room, Carol sank down on the mattress. She was in crisis regarding the gun she was wearing. If she kept the Glock on her person, it would inevitably be found if she was searched thoroughly. Herb Bennett, his manner portentous, had told her she was to meet the Supreme Commander later in the day. "She will interrogate you herself," he said, his tone indicating that Carol should consider this an honor.

Carol suspected that she would be checked over to make sure she was no threat before she would be allowed into the woman's presence. If so, her gun would be discovered.

But if she left it hidden in the cell, she had given up temporarily the one thing that gave her a potent means of escape. And what if the one chance she was presented with occurred when she was being taken to the Supreme Commander?

Was there any possibility they would search the cell while she was out of it? And what if they took her somewhere else, and didn't return her here?

Whichever course she chose, it was a gamble — and if she guessed wrong, the price would be her life.

Four hours later, two armed men came to collect

her. They wore the familiar military fatigues, side arms on their belts, and carried rifles.

"Hands behind your neck," said the one whose manner indicated he was in charge. "Walk in front of us."

"I need to use the bathroom." This was true, but Carol also wanted to reconnoiter every possible escape route.

She was marched into the farmhouse, through the kitchen, and into a hallway. "That's a toilet." The leader gave her a frosty smile. "There's no way out, so don't waste your time looking. You've got two minutes."

He hadn't lied. The only window of the poky little bathroom was high up on the wall and securely boarded over. She used the toilet and, under the noise of flushing water, rapidly checked the cabinets. All were empty: There was nothing that could be used as a weapon.

There was a peremptory knock on the door. "Out of there!"

She was taken to a room in the front of the house, to be ceremonially turned over to what seemed to be an honor guard. A man and a woman came out of the room and stood to attention. "The prisoner. Delivered in good order."

"Face the wall and spread your legs," said the female. She was young, scarcely in her twenties, but her face was hard beyond her years.

She searched Carol comprehensively, then stepped back. "Take off your ring and watch." Carol handed over her opal ring and gold watch. The young woman tucked them into the breast pocket of her tunic.

Buttoning the flap, she said, "The prisoner is clear." Both she and the other guard drew their side arms. "Enter the room."

"I'm sorry to keep you waiting," said Lizbeth Hamilton. "But it was necessary for me to cover the parade for the newspaper. It would have been noticed if I'd been absent."

She looked almost charming in her fatigues, the variegated colors suiting her rich russet hair.

The room was set up as a command center, with one wall covered with diagrams and maps of each Australian state stuck with colored pins. A long table held other maps and documents.

Carol said, "I half expected to see Elaine Cosil-Ross here."

"Elaine and Stuart are patrons of Inner Circle, two of the many who support us." Lizbeth motioned Carol to a metal chair that was set in the middle of the room. "You would be surprised the number of concerned citizens who do."

The two guards took up position on either side of Carol's chair.

"You've already demonstrated you can fight back," said Lizbeth, "and I admire that, of course, but I must point out that if you make any attempt to move, my guards will shoot you. Not to kill — that will come later — but to cause you the maximum pain."

"Why not kill me now, as you're going to anyway."

Lizbeth regarded her with approval. "I see you're not going to grovel. We're not barbarians, Carol. You'll be tried by a properly constituted people's court. If you're found guilty, sentence will be passed.

It's a capital offense, so the death penalty will apply."

"I have a right to know what I'm accused of, I presume?"

"As a member of institutionalized oppression, you betray all free citizens of our country. More, you seek specifically to destroy Inner Circle. And by opposing us, you foil the will of the people."

"Your interpretation of the will of the people."

Lizbeth shook her head, rueful at Carol's intransigence. "*You* are the agent of One World Government. *We* are the true representatives of freedom-loving citizens. As you willingly support the forces of tyranny, you are equally guilty with those that lead you. We have the legal and inalienable right to judge and punish the enemies of the people."

"And this was your justification for the bomb that killed Sergeant Griffin?"

Lizbeth was unmoved by Carol's scorn. "Perhaps you fail to understand we are at war," she said. "Griffin was a threat to our security. He was asking too many questions, getting too close to the truth, so he had to be eliminated. Herb Bennett called him to say someone had left a parcel of old historical records at the pub for him to pick up. We knew he'd be keen to see the contents, but it didn't matter whether Griffin opened it in the car or elsewhere."

"Someone else could have been killed, as well."

Lizbeth shrugged. "There'll always be casualties in war."

"And what did Dean Bayliss and Wayne Bucci do, that you saw fit to execute them?"

"This is a vital time, Carol." Lizbeth's voice swelled with elation. She gestured widely at the maps pinned to the wall. "We are about to strike at the seat of power in each state of our commonwealth. Freedom-loving people will see Operation Liberty as a signal and rise up to destroy their oppressors. These essential blows must be swiftly and ruthlessly delivered, so absolute secrecy is imperative."

It was useless to argue against such fanatical belief, but Carol still said, "What crime had those men committed that could possibly justify death by a firing squad?"

Lizbeth frowned. "I try to explain, and you refuse to listen." Her tone was that of an affronted teacher. "Let me say it again. Their crime was treason against the free citizens of Australia. Bucci was caught in this room, and it was obvious Bayliss was equally guilty because Rick Turner testified that Bayliss had recruited him as a new member. We weren't able to determine if they were in the pay of your corrupt government, but anyone who might reveal Operation Liberty must be eliminated. These men earned their execution, and it was meted out after a fair and full judgment of the court."

Through all this the two guards on either side of Carol had remained silent, but as Lizbeth finished, the male said, "I salute the Inner Circle."

In other circumstances his raw belief would have been amusing. Here it was chilling. Carol struggled to keep her voice even. "What about Kent Agar? Surely he stands for many of the things that you do?"

"Agar," said Lizbeth, her revulsion clear. "He is the worst of all — a quisling, a weakling, a betrayer. He was one of our voices in government, our conduit to corruptions being planned by the New World Order. But when he saw our boldness, our valor, our willingness to risk everything for victory, he became impotent, frightened."

"Why didn't you kill him, too?"

Lizbeth looked at her indulgently. "Carol," she said, "we're not stupid. Kent Agar is our channel into the corrupt authorities that hold us captive. He is, frankly, worth more to Inner Circle alive."

"So you warned him."

"*T* for traitor. A message he could not possibly misunderstand. And to guarantee Kent's silence, I arranged for the medallion his son gave my daughter to be left at the scene." She folded her arms and leaned back against the table. "Kent Agar will come back to us," she said complacently. "His son already hears the call. He has left home and joined us for this great moment in Australia's history."

With an effort, Carol put a note of keen inquiry into her voice. "What is it that Inner Circle will do that is so bold, so courageous?"

The question obviously pleased. "I want you to consider this in the hours you have before your trial . . ." Lizbeth indicated the maps of each state. "The red pins indicate the points where our militia teams will initiate Operation Liberty. They start leaving here tomorrow morning, to ensure each is in place by Wednesday." She smiled in anticipation. "You will not be here to see it, but we will strike simultaneously in each capital city. The means need not concern you, but it will be swift and sure."

"Sarin," said Carol.

Jolted, Lizbeth threw her head back. "How do you know that?" Startled by their leader's vehemence, the two guards moved closer to Carol.

"How do you know that?" Lizbeth repeated.

When Carol remained obstinately silent, Lizbeth stepped forward until she was directly in front of the chair. Lowering her chin to stare directly into Carol's eyes, she said, "I must know exactly what you know. And you will tell me, be very sure of that. Nothing can be allowed to prevent these blows for freedom. I will give you a short time to reflect, and then ask you again. If you refuse, we will make you speak."

She gestured to the two guards. "Put her back in the cell. I will see her again in half an hour."

CHAPTER SIXTEEN

Pushed roughly back into her cell, Carol waited until the padlock clicked shut before rummaging under the mattress. The Glock in its holster was still there. She strapped it on with trembling fingers. She had no doubt that, if she refused to cooperate, Lizbeth Hamilton would stand calmly by and watch her be tortured.

Knowing that it was likely she would be searched again before being allowed in the Supreme Commander's presence, Carol knew that she had to make an attempt to escape when they took her out of the cell.

She prowled around the little room, breathing deeply to ready herself. Without a watch she could only guess at the time. It was early afternoon, and she would have preferred to wait for darkness, but circumstances made that impossible.

She formulated a plan. As before, she expected two militia would escort her to the command room. When they opened the cell door they would be on guard, and then they would make her walk in front of them into the homestead. She'd ask to use the toilet again, conceal the palm-size Glock in her hand, and take her chances at wounding or killing both of them as she came out of the bathroom.

Ten rounds. She took out the gun and checked it again. Nine rounds in the magazine. One in the chamber. She slid it back into the ankle holster. If she could get the two of them with one shot each, she would have eight left. She remembered an instructor's voice: *It's a small target, but a head shot, if you can manage it, will bring them down, fast.*

The metal door vibrated to a heavy blow. "Wakey, wakey, bitch!" It was Rick Turner's sneering voice. "We're coming to get you!"

She stood, weight balanced on her toes, breathing deeply. Sunshine glared in her eyes as the door was flung open. Rick Turner stood there, grinning. He had changed into camouflage fatigues and carried an assault rifle.

"Want to be convinced to talk?" he asked. With one swift movement he stepped into the cell and drove the butt of the rifle into her face.

Carol heard her nose break. She fell back against the wall, pain blossoming in her face like a fiery flower. She bent her knees, grabbed for the Glock.

He stood over her, laughing. He raised the rifle, butt toward her. "Not so beautiful now, are you? Here's another one."

The shot caught him full in the face. He didn't make a sound, but fell as though he was a marionette whose strings had been cut.

"What the hell . . ." The bulk of the other guard filled the doorway, shutting out the light. He looked incredulously at Turner's body, then swung up his rifle. Carol steadied the gun in two hands and fired. He slumped, and sunlight leaped into the room.

Then she was out of the cell and running.

She swerved around the side of the house, sprinting for the vehicles parked there. Someone shouted behind her. A woman came out of the corrugated-iron barn. She gaped at Carol, then went for her side arm.

Squeezing off a desperate shot, Carol missed, the bullet harmlessly striking the metal siding. The woman got her weapon free and fired, but she also failed to hit her target.

Carol was running so fast that she couldn't stop herself from colliding with the side of the first truck. She wrenched open the driver's door. No key in the ignition.

More shouts. Two shots. One hit the ground near her feet, the other struck metal and ricocheted past her face. Her breath sobbing in her throat, Carol ran for the next vehicle, a red Toyota four-wheel drive.

Keys glinted in the steering column. She leaped

in. There was no time to shut the door. The engine fired. As she accelerated, a man, heavy revolver leveled, swung himself up into the cabin.

Carol looked down the barrel of his gun. She wrenched the wheel violently. The Toyota bucked and he was almost thrown off. The shot, earsplitting in the enclosed space, went through the roof.

He hauled himself back and aimed the revolver at her face. She shoved the Glock against his chest and fired. He grunted, his gun wavered, but he didn't let go the frame of the door. She pulled the trigger again. He fell away.

Carol floored the accelerator, the door still swinging open. A volley of shots broke the rear window. She jolted across rough ground, and then hit the smoother surface of the road.

She risked a look behind her. Two vehicles were pursuing. Red was splashing onto her lap. For a moment she thought a bullet had wounded her, but the blood was pouring from her nose.

They were close behind her and gaining. Carol hit the initial curve so fast that she had to fight the wheel to stay on the road. The engine screamed as she rammed down to a lower gear and roared up the first steep slope. She had left the paddocks behind, and wild bush bordered the road.

She glanced in the rearview mirror. They'd fallen back a little. Another corner. Branches thrashed against the side of the vehicle as she skidded off the edge. She wrestled with the wheel and got back on the road.

Another volley of shots. The vehicle slewed to one side and she realized the back tires had been hit. She fought with the wheel, but the four-wheel drive was careening out of control. It left the road, broadsided a tree, then tilted, and gathering speed, lurched down into a steep gully.

Green blurred in front of her; the noise of branches smashing against the windscreen was deafening. It suddenly exploded, showering her with glass.

A huge boulder loomed ahead. Carol was slammed against the steering wheel as the wild ride came to a sudden, jolting halt.

Winded, she fought for breath. In the sudden silence she could hear shouted instructions. She looked at the gun, still clenched tight in her fist. Five rounds left, and then she would be defenseless.

She pulled herself out of the wreck and stumbled over the rocky floor of the gully. She could hear them calling to one another as they came down. They had spread out to cut off her escape.

The other side of the gully was almost vertical. Scrabbling and slipping, she began a desperate climb. Stones and dirt broke loose as she hauled herself up the cliff. A shot rang out. Somebody bellowed, "The Commander wants her alive!"

She looked down and saw that several of her pursuers had begun the ascent after her. Gasping for air, she clawed her way over the rim and got to her feet. A deep chattering sound filled the air. A helicopter appeared, flying low over the treetops. It hovered for a moment, its downdraft lashing the vegetation into a tumult, then tilted and went toward the road. Below her, the men began to scramble down the cliff.

Carol pushed her way through thick bushes, then slumped against a tree. Pain that had been held at a distance during her flight now washed over her in dizzy waves.

She opened her eyes. Far below, Denise's voice was calling her name. "Carol? Where are you? The cavalry's here!"

It seemed a long time before she heard them tramping through the brush toward her. Denise, followed by three uniformed soldiers, came to a halt. She looked at Carol's face. "Carol!"

Carol tried to smile. "That bad, eh?"

Denise knelt beside her. "I'm sorry we took so long. Our scanners intercepted the cell phone calls, so we had a fair idea where you were. Still, it took some time to get a rescue party together." She pried Carol's fingers away from the Glock. "You won't need this any more."

"Lizbeth Hamilton?"

Denise grinned. "Handcuffed and raving. She's taken it very hard that we've confiscated her sarin. It was neatly packed and ready to go."

CHAPTER SEVENTEEN

Carol sighed impatiently. The officious little doctor who had just examined her said he wouldn't be discharging her until the next day. "And you'll be needing plastic surgery on your nose," he said as a bracing final comment.

She had hardly recognized herself in a mirror. She had two black eyes, her face was swollen, and there was a long angry scrape along the side of her jaw.

Although she had two cracked ribs, her face was too painful to touch, and she felt light-headed when she tried to stand, she wanted to be out of this rough-textured hospital gown and into her own familiar clothes and away from this place.

She played with the black opal ring Denise had returned to her, then lay back and inspected the white ceiling. She didn't feel like reading, although Anne and Mark Bourke had brought her magazines. And she certainly didn't feel like eating anything from the elaborate basket of fruit that Madeline had delivered herself before reluctantly returning to Sydney for a "Shipley Report" special on Inner Circle that would undoubtedly garner huge ratings.

Carol's eyes traced the borders of the ceiling where its sterile whiteness met the equally hygienic pallor of the walls. She felt subtly depressed, as though everything in her life had been leached of intensity and meaning. What did she care about? *Who* did she care about? Even David, her son, had a complete life of which she had no part.

"Heavens," said a voice dear in its familiarity. "I can't even leave you for a year, and look at the trouble you get yourself into."

Carol struggled to sit up. Sybil stood at the end of the bed, her red hair blazing against the white background.

Carol's throat tightened. She couldn't speak.

"Don't cry, Carol," Sybil said gently. "It'll ruin your image."

CHRISTABEL by Laura Adams. 224 pp. Two captive hearts and the passion that will set them free.   ISBN 1-56280-214-3 $11.95

PRIVATE PASSIONS by Laura DeHart Young. 192 pp. An unforgettable new portrait of lesbian love . . .   ISBN 1-56280-215-1   11.95

BAD MOON RISING by Barbara Johnson. 208 pp. 2nd Colleen Fitzgerald mystery.   ISBN 1-56280-211-9   11.95

RIVER QUAY by Janet McClellan. 208 pp. 3rd Tru North mystery.   ISBN 1-56280-212-7   11.95

ENDLESS LOVE by Lisa Shapiro. 272 pp. To believe, once again, that love can be forever.   ISBN 1-56280-213-5   11.95

FALLEN FROM GRACE by Pat Welch. 256 pp. 6th Helen Black mystery.   ISBN 1-56280-209-7   11.95

THE NAKED EYE by Catherine Ennis. 208 pp. Her lover in the camera's eye . . .   ISBN 1-56280-210-0   11.95

OVER THE LINE by Tracey Richardson. 176 pp. 2nd Stevie Houston mystery.   ISBN 1-56280-202-X   11.95

JULIA'S SONG by Ann O'Leary. 208 pp. Strangely disturbing . . . strangely exciting.   ISBN 1-56280-197-X   11.95

LOVE IN THE BALANCE by Marianne K. Martin. 256 pp. Weighing the costs of love . . .   ISBN 1-56280-199-6   11.95

PIECE OF MY HEART by Julia Watts. 208 pp. All the stuff that dreams are made of —   ISBN 1-56280-206-2   11.95

MAKING UP FOR LOST TIME by Karin Kallmaker. 240 pp. Nobody does it better . . .   ISBN 1-56280-196-1   11.95

GOLD FEVER by Lyn Denison. 224 pp. By author of *Dream Lover.*   ISBN 1-56280-201-1   11.95

WHEN THE DEAD SPEAK by Therese Szymanski. 224 pp. 2nd Brett Higgins mystery.   ISBN 1-56280-198-8   11.95

FOURTH DOWN by Kate Calloway. 240 pp. 4th Cassidy James
mystery.   ISBN 1-56280-205-4   11.95

A MOMENT'S INDISCRETION by Peggy J. Herring. 176 pp.
There's a fine line between love and lust . . .   ISBN 1-56280-194-5   11.95

CITY LIGHTS/COUNTRY CANDLES by Penny Hayes. 208 pp.
About the women she has known . . .   ISBN 1-56280-195-3   11.95

POSSESSIONS by Kaye Davis. 240 pp. 2nd Maris Middleton
mystery.   ISBN 1-56280-192-9   11.95

A QUESTION OF LOVE by Saxon Bennett. 208 pp. Every
woman is granted one great love.   ISBN 1-56280-205-4   11.95

RHYTHM TIDE by Frankie J. Jones. 160 pp.   . . . to desire
passionately and be passionately desired.   ISBN 1-56280-189-9   11.95

PENN VALLEY PHOENIX by Janet McClellan. 208 pp. 2nd
Tru North Mystery.   ISBN 1-56280-200-3   11.95

BY RESERVATION ONLY by Jackie Calhoun. 240 pp. A
chance for true happiness.   ISBN 1-56280-191-0   11.95

OLD BLACK MAGIC by Jaye Maiman. 272 pp. 9th Robin
Miller mystery.   ISBN 1-56280-175-9   11.95

LEGACY OF LOVE by Marianne K. Martin. 240 pp. Women
will do anything for her . . .   ISBN 1-56280-184-8   11.95

LETTING GO by Ann O'Leary. 160 pp. Laura, at 39, in love
with 23-year-old Kate.   ISBN 1-56280-183-X   11.95

LADY BE GOOD edited by Barbara Grier and Christine Cassidy.
288 pp. Erotic stories by Naiad Press authors.   ISBN 1-56280-180-5   14.95

CHAIN LETTER by Claire McNab. 288 pp. 9th Carol Ashton
mystery.   ISBN 1-56280-181-3   11.95

NIGHT VISION by Laura Adams. 256 pp. Erotic fantasy romance
by "famous" author.   ISBN 1-56280-182-1   11.95

SEA TO SHINING SEA by Lisa Shapiro. 256 pp. Unable to resist
the raging passion . . .   ISBN 1-56280-177-5   11.95

THIRD DEGREE by Kate Calloway. 224 pp. 3rd Cassidy James
mystery.   ISBN 1-56280-185-6   11.95

WHEN THE DANCING STOPS by Therese Szymanski. 272 pp.
1st Brett Higgins mystery.   ISBN 1-56280-186-4   11.95

PHASES OF THE MOON by Julia Watts. 192 pp. . . . . hungry
for everything life has to offer.   ISBN 1-56280-176-7   11.95

BABY IT'S COLD by Jaye Maiman. 256 pp. 5th Robin Miller
mystery.   ISBN 1-56280-156-2   10.95

CLASS REUNION by Linda Hill. 176 pp. The girl from her
past . . .   ISBN 1-56280-178-3   11.95

DREAM LOVER by Lyn Denison. 224 pp. A soft, sensuous,
romantic fantasy.   ISBN 1-56280-173-1   11.95

FORTY LOVE by Diana Simmonds. 288 pp. Joyous, heart-warming romance.   ISBN 1-56280-171-6   11.95

IN THE MOOD by Robbi Sommers. 160 pp. The queen of erotic tension!   ISBN 1-56280-172-4   11.95

SWIMMING CAT COVE by Lauren Douglas. 192 pp. 2nd Allison O'Neil Mystery.   ISBN 1-56280-168-6   11.95

THE LOVING LESBIAN by Claire McNab and Sharon Gedan. 240 pp. Explore the experiences that make lesbian love unique.
ISBN 1-56280-169-4   14.95

COURTED by Celia Cohen. 160 pp. Sparkling romantic encounter.   ISBN 1-56280-166-X   11.95

SEASONS OF THE HEART by Jackie Calhoun. 240 pp. Romance through the years.   ISBN 1-56280-167-8   11.95

K. C. BOMBER by Janet McClellan. 208 pp. 1st Tru North mystery.   ISBN 1-56280-157-0   11.95

LAST RITES by Tracey Richardson. 192 pp. 1st Stevie Houston mystery.   ISBN 1-56280-164-3   11.95

EMBRACE IN MOTION by Karin Kallmaker. 256 pp. A whirlwind love affair.   ISBN 1-56280-165-1   11.95

HOT CHECK by Peggy J. Herring. 192 pp. Will workaholic Alice fall for guitarist Ricky?   ISBN 1-56280-163-5   11.95

OLD TIES by Saxon Bennett. 176 pp. Can Cleo surrender to a passionate new love?   ISBN 1-56280-159-7   11.95

LOVE ON THE LINE by Laura DeHart Young. 176 pp. Will Stef win Kay's heart?   ISBN 1-56280-162-7   11.95

DEVIL'S LEG CROSSING by Kaye Davis. 192 pp. 1st Maris Middleton mystery.   ISBN 1-56280-158-9   11.95

COSTA BRAVA by Marta Balletbo Coll. 144 pp. Read the book, see the movie!   ISBN 1-56280-153-8   11.95

MEETING MAGDALENE & OTHER STORIES by Marilyn Freeman. 144 pp. Read the book, see the movie!
ISBN 1-56280-170-8   11.95

SECOND FIDDLE by Kate 208 pp. 2nd P.I. Cassidy James mystery.   ISBN 1-56280-169-6   11.95

These are just a few of the many Naiad Press titles — we are the oldest and largest lesbian/feminist publishing company in the world. We also offer an enormous selection of lesbian video products. Please request a complete catalog. We offer personal service; we encourage and welcome direct mail orders from individuals who have limited access to bookstores carrying our publications.

LOOKING FOR NAIAD?

Buy our books at
www.naiadpress.com

or call our toll-free number
1-800-533-1973

or by fax (24 hours a day)
1-850-539-9731